HEARTACHE HOSPITAL

Staff Nurse Jessica Brook has known and loved
Clive Mortimer ever since she started nursing
at Hartlake Hospital. But the action she takes,
after seeing him fooling around with a first-year
nurse again, means that Hartlake turns quickly
into Heartache Hospital . . .

HEARTACHE HOSPITAL

BY

LYNNE COLLINS

MILLS & BOON LIMITED
London . Sydney . Toronto

First published in Great Britain 1981
by Mills & Boon Limited, 15–16 Brook's Mews,
London W1A 1DR

© Lynne Collins 1981

Australian copyright 1981
Philippine copyright 1981

ISBN 0 263 73460 9

Set in 10 on 11½ pt Monophoto Plantin

Made and printed in Great Britain by
Richard Clay (The Chaucer Press) Ltd.,
Bungay, Suffolk

CHAPTER ONE

THE ward was peaceful. All the patients were asleep, even the nineteen-year-old recovering from a motorcycle accident who liked to flirt with the junior nurses at an hour when he believed their resistance to be low. Only the previous night, Jessica had caught him in the kitchen, balancing precariously on his crutches while embracing the slender waist of a nurse who made little effort to avoid being kissed. She had sent him back to bed and scolded pretty Nurse Flynn for encouraging the lad but she knew from her own experience that fending off flirtation was an occupational hazard. Indeed, when a male patient had been very ill or badly injured in an accident, it was a welcome sign of recovery if he began to take notice of the nurses.

Jessica stood at the office window and looked over the sleeping ward. For some reason, she was uneasy. Men's Surgical was usually busy and she had some very sick patients on the ward. But she had just made her round and everything seemed to be satisfactory. So why was every instinct alerting her for action?

Perhaps she was just tired. She sat down at the desk to write up her report, stifling a yawn. She had spent most of the previous day shopping for an outfit for Suzy's wedding instead of sleeping. She was going to miss Suzy. They had been friends since the first day that both had arrived at Hartlake to begin their training. It seemed a very long time ago now—and how green they had been!

Remembering her own early days, Jessica tried to be sympathetic towards the new juniors although it did not do to be lenient with them. Strict discipline was part of the system and it was a very necessary part of a nurse's training. How she and Suzy had suffered at the hands of their seniors when they first went on the wards! Weary and forlorn and with that awful feeling of always being rushed off their feet and never having enough time for anything, they had vowed every day to give up nursing. But they had stuck it out, even enjoying much of it, and finally had achieved the accolade for which they had worked so hard and so long— the badge of a State Registered Nurse.

Now Suzy was giving it all up to be a farmer's wife. Ian was a lovely fellow and they were very much in love. Jessica wished them happy but it did seem a terrible waste of all that training and she was afraid that Suzy would be bored to tears in the Yorkshire Dales, so far from all her friends and missing all the excitement of nursing.

Jessica was not against marriage. In fact, she would like very much to be married, she thought, a trifle wistfully, a certain man and his elusiveness leaping to mind. But she had no intention of giving up nursing as soon as the ring was on her finger, like too many girls. She loved it too much and nurses were in such short supply that she would feel guilty about deserting the patients!

Nurse Flynn erupted into the office without knocking. 'Can I go for my dinner now, Staff?'

She was a very pretty girl with the dancing eyes and impish smile of the Irish but she was never tidy and she was a scatterbrain. Full of good intentions but forgetful. Jessica regarded her with something akin to despair.

'Straighten your cap, nurse—and just look at that apron! What have you been doing? You look like a female edition of Just William!' The girl chuckled, delighted. 'No, it isn't funny, nurse,' Jessica said swiftly, severely. 'Making messes in the kitchen is for little girls. You are a grown woman learning to care for the sick. If I was a patient on this ward, your present appearance and general behaviour wouldn't inspire me with much confidence. Go to your meal and make sure you are clean and tidy when you report back to me!'

'Yes, Staff . . . thank you, Staff.'

With the closed door between them, Amanda stuck out her tongue and then danced along the corridor towards the swing doors of the ward, quite un-chastened. They were pushed wide just as she reached them by a tall, good-looking man in a white coat. He smiled, his dark eyes crinkling in the way that caused every impressionable nurse at Hartlake Hospital to declare that Clive Mortimer was an attractive devil!

He smiled but he did not speak. Very junior nurses were probably beneath his notice, Amanda decided, a little resentfully. She watched him walk along to the office, knock lightly and enter. Jessica Brook was in love with him, everyone said, but judging by her sharp-tongued mood of the moment it seemed that the course of true love was not running too smoothly . . .

Jessica glanced up from the report as the door opened. 'Oh, hallo,' she said, relaxing but slightly cool.

Clive raised an amused eyebrow. 'That isn't much of a welcome.'

She smiled. 'Sorry. I'm a bit on edge.'

He bestowed a light kiss on the shining blonde hair that was drawn into a severe knot on the nape of her neck. He knew how beautiful she could be with that mass of hair loosened and falling about her face, her eyes warm and her mouth tender, her whole being softened with loving. He knew how sweet and gentle and ardent she could be in his embrace . . . this cool, efficient and ambitious young woman who gave the juniors the impression that she was a cold-blooded martinet. 'Problems?'

'None at all. That's why I'm edgy. It isn't natural,' she said wryly.

'Count your blessings, my sweet.' His hand resting lightly on her shoulder, he glanced over the report. 'Mm . . . I'm glad to see that Wyatt is rallying. I was a little concerned. And Benson is responding to that new drug, I see. That's good. The old man wasn't too happy about trying it but I thought it might do the trick in this case. This young man, Wood. He seems to be getting on nicely.'

'With my nurses, certainly,' she said tartly. 'Particularly the Flynn girl!'

Clive tickled the nape of her neck with his long fingers. 'Don't be such an old dragon. I can remember when you were young and flighty,' he teased.

'I didn't flirt with the patients!'

'No,' he agreed, smiling. 'Only with medical students. Patients come and go, don't they? Doctors stay for ever—some of us!'

There was just a trace of bitternesss in his tone. Jessica looked up quickly. 'Oh, Clive—no luck?'

He had applied for the post of Registrar at another hospital and he had been confident of getting it. He had all the right qualifications. But Sir Lionel did not wish to part with a very promising assistant and Clive suspected that his boss had dropped a word in a certain ear. 'Not this time.'

8

Jessica touched his hand gently. 'I'm sorry.'

He shrugged. 'Just as well, perhaps. This place would never run so well without me.'

'You would be missed, certainly.' The softening of her tone implied that he would be a personal loss. She had loved him since the days when they had both been raw students at Hartlake—and she hoped that one day he would admit to loving her. But it seemed that career came before everything else where Clive was concerned.

'Oh, I don't know. Some people would be very glad to see the back of me,' he said dryly.

'Yes, I daresay. Brilliant young doctors are not always popular with their colleagues,' she said lightly, eyes twinkling.

He laughed. 'You're a tonic, Nurse Brook! No wonder all your patients are doing so well!' He bent to kiss her. Her lips were warm and sweet and swiftly responsive and he knew the stirring of desire that she could evoke so easily. 'What night are you off? We'll have dinner and celebrate not getting the job at the Central.'

'Friday—and Suzy's wedding is on Saturday,' she reminded him.

'Yes, of course. It's your free weekend! Great! We'll spend it together, my sweet—and make wonderful whoopee!' His dark eyes were full of laughing promise. She smiled but shook her head. He sobered suddenly. 'It's ages since you went out with me, Jess—much too long.'

'We've both been busy,' she said carefully.

He looked down at her thoughtfully. 'I suspect you've been consulting the Agony Aunties,' he said lightly. ' "Keep him at a distance and he'll come running, my dear . . ." That is what you're doing these days, isn't it?'

Her eyes danced. 'Is it?'

'I'm bloody sure it is!'

'It could be . . . another man!' She lowered her voice dramatically on the last words.

He grinned. 'I'd know about it,' he said confidently.

She sighed. 'That's true. There's no such thing as a private life at Hartlake!' She rose to her feet. 'Would you like some tea?'

'No, I must get on. I don't suppose all the wards are as quiet as this one.' He moved to the door. 'I'll pick you up at eight on Friday—okay?'

'Yes. But don't plan on making a night of it, Clive,' she warned firmly. 'I want to look my best for the wedding.'

He smiled wryly. 'I'm getting the message—loud and clear!'

As the door closed, Jessica sighed again, a little ruefully. He was too perceptive. She *had* been playing hard to get just lately in the hope that he would realise just how important she was to him—and she had the dreadful feeling that she was not very important after all.

Clive was ambitious and dedicated and quite determined not to make a lasting commitment to any woman just yet. Because of that reluctance to become too involved there had been other girls in his life. But he always came back to Jessica between affairs. Loving him, she had learned to accept—and because her own career mattered so much, she had almost been grateful for the occasional breathing space in their relationship. Loving could be very demanding and very distracting.

But one could not go on in that way for ever—and

perhaps Suzy's dewy-eyed happiness of recent weeks had emphasised the emptiness of her own personal life. She felt that Clive ought not to keep her dangling on a string any longer. Either he loved her and wished to marry her and should say so and give her some hope for the future—or he was incapable of loving her enough and should say so and free her from hoping. Then she could forget the foolish dream of husband, home and children for the time being and concentrate wholeheartedly on nursing . . .

Amanda Flynn came back to the ward in a clean apron and with a deceptively demure manner. Jessica sent the other junior to have her meal and the night continued on its unusually placid way. With that faint uneasiness still troubling her, she made another round of the ward.

Nicky Wood slept the sleep of the innocent, looking ridiculously young for all his nineteen years. Mr Wyatt in Bed 3 had caused some concern immediately after his operation for a perforated gastric ulcer but was now doing nicely and old Mr Benson with his collapsed lung following a nasty bout of pneumonia and pleurisy was doing very much better than anyone had expected, considering his advanced age. Jim Carver, the licensee of the pub that was so well frequented by the medical students, was recovering well from an emergency operation for peritonitis. He had collapsed in the saloon bar, a classic textbook case for the benefit of the students he was serving at the time.

Jessica paused at the foot of one bed. She had been taught in the early days of training that a good nurse should not allow her personal feelings to affect her work but she could not always be as detached as hospital life demanded. Mr Irving in Bed 12 was very like her father, both in looks and personality, and she took a special interest in him.

He had come in for an investigatory operation and Sir Lionel had discovered an inoperable cancer. He had consulted his G.P. too late and had only a few months at most to live but was cheerful and quite un-complaining and full of optimistic plans for the future. A retired teacher, he had no wife or children but there was no lack of telephone enquiries, of flowers and small gifts and it was obvious that he was loved and respected by friends and neighbours and ex-pupils. He was a favourite on the ward, too ... with staff and patients alike. Very soon, he would be transferred to a local hospice that cared for terminal cases and Jessica knew that he would be much missed.

She suddenly sensed that he was awake and she moved to the side of the bed. 'Is there anything that you want?' she asked quietly.

'No, thank you, nurse. I'm quite comfortable.'

'Any pain?'

'None at all. You mustn't worry about me, my dear,' he said gently. 'I'm just a fraud, you know— taking up too much of everyone's time.'

'Would you like a hot drink?' She glanced at her watch. 'I expect Nurse Flynn is switching on the kettle for my cuppa at this very moment. I'm sure you won't say no to some tea.'

He smiled and patted her hand. 'Ah, I'm afraid you know my little weakness. But this is spoiling me, nurse.'

On her way down the ward, Jessica was hailed by a loud whisper from another bed. 'Did I hear you men-tion tea, love. I could use a cup.'

It was the young window-cleaner who had slipped

and fallen from a wet window-sill, fracturing his skull. He had undergone emergency surgery to relieve pressure on the brain and had lain in a coma for some days. Frantic with worry, his heavily-pregnant wife had spent long hours at his bedside and the medical students had laid bets on the chances that she would be the first person to give birth in Men's Surgical. Certainly she had left it almost too late to admit that she was in labour—and Elvis Palmer had eventually woken to the news that his wife and son were in the Maternity Unit of the same hospital.

He was doing well and looked forward to the daily visits from his wife with news of the thriving baby. But there was some concern about brain damage affecting his right arm and leg and his speech was slightly slurred. By day he was a lively member of the ward, refusing to worry, reassuring his young wife and talking confidently of the future. But at night that confidence deserted him and he liked to talk, needing reassurance in his turn. He found a sympathetic listener in Jessica when she could find the time for she liked the young man who was so much in love, so anxious about his family.

She paused briefly to speak to him, to promise a cup of tea, and then went on towards the kitchen. A flashing light on the high panel at the end of the ward stopped her in her tracks. She swung round, suddenly alert to danger. It was Mr Irving's light that flashed in response to his touch on the call-button and she sped to his bedside. He waved her away before she could reach him. 'Not me . . . young Elvis!' he said urgently.

Moments before, the young man had been alert and cheerful. Now he was obviously in the throes of a totally unexpected cardiac arrest. Instinctively Jessica

13

reacted to the emergency. She flashed the red light that would bring Amanda Flynn swiftly to her assistance and ran to the house telephone to dial 999 to alert the cardiac arrest team. Then she hurried back to begin external heart massage until the team of experts should arrive. She would not admit that it might already be too late, that Elvis Palmer had died within seconds of that massive heart attack. If any amount of effort and prayer could revive him then she would not cease to work and pray until the team arrived.

As always, they were amazingly prompt on the scene. But it proved to be too late in this case. They worked on the young man for twenty minutes before finally admitting defeat.

Jessica was shattered. In six years as a nurse she had seen many deaths, known many tragedies. To protect herself, a nurse had to acquire an extra skin and accept the limitations of medical science and surgical skill. But Elvis Palmer had been doing well despite the threat of permanent brain damage. There had been no anxiety about the state of his heart. Perhaps a post-mortem would reveal something that had failed to show on the electrocardiograph. But there seemed no apparent reason for his death.

It had been incredibly sudden and swift. Moments before, she had been with him, talking to him—and she was a trained nurse! How could she have missed the warning signs of an impending heart attack? How could he have died in those few seconds when her back was turned? Shocked and upset, she could not help feeling that she must be to blame in some way. There had to be indications that she had overlooked. She might have saved him if she had been less concerned with her cup of tea and more alert for danger signals!

Hadn't she been troubled by that inexplicable sixth sense all night?

Behind the screening curtains, the sense of urgency slowly evaporated. They could do no more and the team began to collect and tidy their equipment. Soon they would be standing by in readiness for the next emergency.

Lester Thorn, senior doctor on the team that night, looked curiously at the staff nurse who seemed so shocked and bewildered. He noticed that her eyes were brimming with tears. He continued to disconnect the electrodes of the resuscitator from the patient's chest, wondering. He was used to impersonality and brisk efficiency in senior nurses and it could not be the first time that she had lost a patient while she was in charge of a ward.

No one liked to lose a patient. But medicine held that kind of challenge. Win a few, lose a few. No one could ever predict what would happen in a hospital. Occasionally he could perform a miracle with the aid of his machine and bring the seemingly-dead back to life. But this was obviously not his night for a miracle.

He unplugged the resuscitator. 'Sorry,' he said. 'It was too late when we got here, I guess.'

'Yes.' Jessica pulled herself together with a visible effort. The blunt reply must have sounded like an accusation, she realised. He had done his best. Everyone on the team had carried out his particular duty with highly-trained skill and efficiency. As for herself—well, if she had missed a vital warning then surely she had atoned by doing all she could to make that stubborn heart beat again. 'You were very quick,' she said, with more warmth. 'It was just . . . hopeless.'

'Oh, it's never hopeless. All we need is the smallest

spark. It just wasn't there this time.'

Jessica managed a smile. 'Thanks for trying.'

'All in a night's work.' Thrusting back the curtains, he wheeled the machine into the corridor, in the wake of his colleagues. But that smile, flickering so briefly, had triggered a memory. On an impulse, he went back. 'I know you, don't I? You run around with Clive Mortimer.'

She stiffened, abruptly disliking him without reason except that it did not seem the moment to introduce personalities. 'Do I?' Her tone would have chilled a snowman.

Without intending to offend, Lester did not realise she was offended. 'On and off, anyway,' he conceded lightly. 'You don't remember but we have met.'

'I *don't* remember.' Her tone implied that she had no wish to remember.

'Meet me for a drink later and I'll refresh your memory . . . one-thirty in the Kingfisher.' He nodded to her with cheerful self-assurance and strolled back to trundle his machine from the ward.

Jessica looked after him, annoyed. She was used to the casual camaraderie between senior staff, seldom extended to the juniors, but that was taking things too far! The arrogance of the man! Perhaps he was one of Clive's many friends but that did not give him an automatic right to her company! She did not know him and felt no desire to further a very brief acquaintance!

Seething, she busied herself with necessary tasks— and it was some time before she realised that a brief exchange with an over-confident registrar had lifted her out of the disastrous pit of self-blame and depression. The commotion had disturbed the entire ward

16

and it took time to soothe and reassure all the patients. Some went back to sleep immediately. Others could not settle. The rest of the night proved to be as busy and demanding as Jessica had anticipated.

Mr Irving was sorrowing, even bitter, when she reached him. 'It should have been me,' he said sadly.

It was unprofessional but the same thought had sprung to Jessica's mind. For the elderly teacher had very little time left to him and his death that night would have been a merciful release. Elvis Palmer had been young, virile and full of health until his accident. His untimely death was a tragedy for his wife and small son. Life could be very cruel and quite inexplicable at times, Jessica thought wryly.

'You mustn't even think along those lines,' she said briskly. 'Sometimes it's difficult to accept, to understand why such things happen. But we have to believe that all life and death has a purpose.'

He would not be comforted. 'That poor girl,' he said, shaking his head. 'That poor, poor girl . . .'

The whole ward was depressed. But Jessica knew from past experience that spirits would lift with the arrival of a new patient. A hospital was a small and compact world with an almost theatrical unreality about it at times. Jessica sometimes thought that if it was true that all the world's a stage and the people in it merely players, then nowhere did it seem so apt as in a hospital with its drama and excitement, its constantly-changing cast, its tragic and its comic moments, the enormous amount of organisation behind the scenes.

The exit of a player, whether through death or discharge, signalled the entry of another to provide a transient interest and erase thoughts of the departed.

A man could occupy a bed and the attention of staff and fellow-patients for weeks, feeling very much a part of the exclusive hospital community, only to discover on discharge that a return visit to the ward made him feel like an intruder, barely remembered and of only simulated interest. He was no longer the star of his particular drama.

Few patients made the mistake of coming back, in fact. Fewer still gave any thought to nurses and doctors to whom they had been so grateful once they set foot in the outside world once more. And Jessica firmly believed that it was just as it should be. Letters and gifts from grateful patients were heart-warming, of course. But there was so much job-satisfaction in nursing that she felt it was sufficient reward to watch them walk from the ward with regained health.

Thankfully, she handed over the reins to Sister Percival and went off duty. Weary and a little low in spirits, she drove her small car through the maddening morning traffic to the tall, rather shabby house in a side-street, two miles from the hospital. She had a flat on the top floor, two small rooms and a tiny kitchen that was her own and very private domain.

Her immediate neighbour, a fellow-nurse, came hurtling down the narrow stairs just as Jessica prepared to climb the last flight.

'I'm late!' Liz declared, quite unnecessarily. 'Still standing, is it? What kind of night did you have?' She did not wait for an answer. 'See you later . . .'

Jessica smiled wryly as she inserted her key in the lock. That was the worst of night duty. It was an upside-down existence. She was just going to bed as everyone else was beginning the day—and it played havoc with one's social life . . .

CHAPTER TWO

IT was four o'clock when Jessica woke from a long and dreamless sleep. She stirred, stretched in drowsy comfort. Then she knelt on the bed and drew back the heavy curtains. She had gone to bed that morning when the sky was very blue and the sun was shining with the promise of a lovely day. Now, with the usual predictability of April, it was raining and the sky was overcast.

She leaned on the sill and studied the wet rooves and dingy chimney-pots and wondered if it would be wet for the wedding. The sun would shine for Suzy and Ian, no matter what the weather was like, of course. But the thin silk suit she had bought to wear would almost dissolve in rain, she thought wryly.

She was glad it was Friday, at last. She had not enjoyed the last few nights on Currie. She had left the ward that morning with an unmistakable feeling of relief.

She had said goodbye to Mr Irving with a pang for he was being transferred to the hospice and they would not meet again. She had said goodbye to Nicky Wood, well enough to be discharged that day, and firmly refused the kiss he had cheekily requested. She had said goodbye to Mr Wyatt and old Mr Benson and told Jim Carver that she would soon see him in the Kingfisher, back behind the bar serving his customers. She had said goodbye to all the patients who had been of first importance during the busy nights and wondered, as she paused by the bed that Elvis Palmer had occupied and which now contained another young man who had been hurt in a works accident, if she would ever cease to feel a little doubt at the back of her mind. Could she have saved Elvis Palmer? Had she overlooked something of vital importance? She would never know.

Her turn of night duty was finished for the time being. On Tuesday morning she would report to a new ward—and she meant to enjoy the intervening days. There was the evening with Clive to come, the wedding, the opportunity to see all her particular friends and catch up on all the gossip. Very soon she would be involved with the personalities and problems of another group of patients and those in Currie would be relegated to the back of her mind. She was far from being heartless but a good nurse knew what to forget and what to remember. And it was very important to live a full life outside the hospital precincts. If she did not, her work, and the patients, would eventually suffer.

She was ready when Clive came for her that evening and she ran down to his waiting car at the first sound of the horn, a little flush of excitement in her cheeks, her heart beating with betraying rapidity. He smiled and leaned from the driving seat to open the car door and she slipped into the seat beside him.

He kissed her so carelessly that her heart sank. Would she ever know how much he cared about her? Sometimes she believed that he came close to loving her as she loved him. Sometimes she felt that she was little more than a very good friend to him. Sometimes he was an ardent and tender lover, filling her with happiness and hope. Sometimes, like this evening, he was cool, hurtfully casual. A man of moods ... and

Jessica often wondered if she really knew the man she loved. It was so treacherously easy to deceive oneself, to attribute qualities that did not really exist, to blind oneself to faults and failings. She had known and loved Clive for six years. At times, he seemed a stranger.

'You're looking very beautiful,' he said lightly, setting the car in motion. 'New dress?'

'Old dress,' she corrected. 'You've seen it a dozen times.' She was not impatient, too used to his poor memory for such details.

'New face?' he suggested teasingly.

Jessica laughed, spirits lifting. He was dear, familiar, amusing and very lovable Clive—always the same, in truth. It was she who was changeable and difficult and demanding, expecting far too much of him!

She helped him out. 'New hair-style.' She had swept her blonde hair to one side of her head in the newest fashion and although she was not sure that she liked it, Liz had approved—and Clive's flattering words implied that the change of style was an improvement.

Clive turned his head to study her as they paused at traffic lights. 'So it is. Yes, I like it.' He smiled suddenly, warmly. 'I'm glad you decided to let your hair down tonight.'

She could not mistake the meaning behind the words or that particular glow in his dark eyes. 'Don't take anything for granted,' she said with mock severity but she melted inside at the mere thought of his arms about her, his lips on her own. 'Where are we going, anyway?' she asked, mildly curious.

'I did plan a show and a late supper. Then we were

invited to a party and I thought you'd enjoy that. More of a change,' he said smoothly. In fact, he had accepted the invitation and only afterwards remembered the date with Jessica.

She was a little wary, remembering parties in the past given by lively medical students. There was usually a kind of punch it was wiser not to sample, some nameless wine, plenty of beer, very little food and too many people. She would have chosen the show and the supper, an intimate evening and Clive's undivided attention. But he liked a party.

'Anyone I know?' Clive had so many friends, so many acquaintances. She could not know them all.

'Lester Thorn. I'm not sure if you do know him, actually.'

She shook her head. 'The name doesn't ring a bell. What does he do?'

'Assistant Registrar ... Wilmot's team.'

She gave a mock groan. 'That means you'll talk shop all evening, I suppose.'

'We don't have to go,' he said promptly, obligingly, knowing her very well. She would not deny him anything that she thought he wanted.

She smiled, slipped her hand through his arm. 'I haven't been to a party for ages, Clive. It will be fun . . .'

Just as expected, the house was ablaze with lights and the sound of music assaulted their ears from halfway down the narrow street where Clive finally found space to park his car. Entering the open door of the house, they picked their way through the bodies that sat and lounged in the tiny hallway. Most of the staircase was occupied. The entire house was swarming with people, some familiar, some strange, all well-supplied with drinks and in happy party mood.

Clive had brought some bottles with him, like a good friend, and he left Jessica to push his way through to the kitchen where the bar had been set up. She reconciled herself to seeing him again much later in the evening and looked about her for a familiar face.

Someone thrust a drink into her hand. It looked and smelled like the all-too-familiar punch beloved of medical students and she decided not to drink it.

It was not really her kind of party, she realised, and rather too unsophisticated for Clive's taste, she thought. She was surprised that he had chosen to bring her to this type of affair when it was so long since they had enjoyed an evening on their own.

She edged her way through the crowd, nodding and smiling and trying to talk to various people. But someone had turned the stereo to its fullest pitch and the music combined with the ceaseless babble of talk and laughter made it almost impossible to carry on an intelligent conversation.

Eventually, Jessica found a comparatively quiet corner and stood on her own, nursing the glass of punch, waiting for Clive. She knew that she was not going to enjoy the evening when she suddenly saw him in the doorway with an arm around Amanda Flynn, his head bent to murmur something into an obviously receptive ear.

She pinned a smile to her lips, trying not to mind. It meant nothing, of course. It was the kind of thing that happened at parties. Clive had merely been side-tracked on his way to join her and would shake off the girl in a moment or two.

Someone loomed in front of her, tall and masculine, blocking her view of Clive and the junior nurse. 'You stood me up,' Lester said cheerfully, without reproach.

Startled, Jessica did not immediately recognise him. 'Sorry . . .?'

'We had a date for Tuesday. One-thirty in the Kingfisher,' he reminded her lightly. 'You didn't turn up.'

'Oh . . .!' She suddenly recalled the traumatic circumstances of their encounter on the ward and the offensive arrogance of the man who had assumed that she would leap at an invitation. 'I never gave it another thought,' she said coolly. *Or you*, her tone implied.

'You should have made a note on your apron,' he said, smiling. 'However, we had to meet again sooner or later. Hartlake is a close community.'

'That can be a disadvantage,' she said, rather pointedly. He was much too sure of himself! Just because they happened to be in the same line of business, it didn't give him the right to regard her as an old friend—or a promising new one!

Lester regarded her thoughtfully and with interest. The cool manner matched the cool loveliness of hair and skin and eyes. But he remembered a smile . . . a certain smile that hinted at enchanting, tantalising warmth. A smile to remember. A girl to remember, he thought abruptly, recalling the sharp sense of disappointment when she had failed to meet him. He very much wanted to know more of this elusive girl, he decided.

'What do you think of the party?'

Lester was the host, in fact. He had planned a small affair for a few friends, hoping that Clive would bring along the blonde girl who seemed to be the most regular of his girl-friends—and it had suddenly snowballed! The house was bursting at the seams and he did not know two-thirds of his guests. But he did not mind now that he had found the girl with the haunting smile. Even if she was refusing to smile at him!

'Noisy,' she said with feeling.

Lester laughed. 'You aren't enjoying it. If you were the noise wouldn't bother you,' he said with the voice of experience. 'Perhaps you need another drink.'

'I'm still waiting for the first one,' she returned dryly.

He indicated the glass in her hand. 'What's that?'

'I dread to think! It looks and smells very suspicious! It isn't mine. Someone wanted to be rid of it, obviously.'

He took the glass, tasted the contents and grimaced. 'Something that passes for punch, I think.'

'Made with surgical spirit, no doubt. I made the mistake of trying punch at one party in my first year. Never again!' She shuddered at the memory.

Lester smiled. 'Let me get you somthing else. What do you like?' Looking down at her, the smile suddenly deepened in his very blue eyes. Jessica, indifferent, did not notice. 'I'm afraid this isn't your scene,' he said gently.

She shook her head, peered round his tall frame in search of Clive. He was not to be seen and she was troubled. Instinctively, she looked for Amanda Flynn and felt relief as she saw the girl dancing with her arms around another man.

Her spirits rose. She had made too much of a trifling incident. No doubt Clive was looking for her in the crowd. 'Excuse me,' she said, not looking at the tall man who blocked her path. 'I think someone is looking for me . . .'

Lester watched as she eased her way to the door. Then he turned to some friends, his heart sinking. She was not interested in him. Well, he was not so conceited that he expected every woman to respond at a smile, a word, a touch of the hand. Women did respond very often—but this time he was out of luck. It was just one of those things. She was in love with Clive Mortimer if rumour was to be believed. So—forget her! Even if there was something wholly unforgettable about her . . .

Jessica touched Clive's arm as he turned from the makeshift bar with drinks. He smiled and bent to kiss her lightly on the lips. She backed away, not liking a public show of affection, although it was doubtful if anyone had taken the least notice. There was always a lot of kissing and cuddling at parties.

'Enjoying it, darling? Great party, isn't it?' Clive spoke absently, looking over her head. 'I promised this drink to someone. Now I can't see her anywhere . . .'

Jessica's heart contracted with a familiar pain. She knew him so well, knew all the signs that his fickle fancy had been caught by a pretty face, a flirtatious manner. 'I expect you mean Amanda Flynn,' she said with commendable casualness. 'She's dancing.'

Clive was never sure if her tolerance stemmed from lack of jealousy or commonsense. Perhaps she just knew that he always came back to her, for all his wanderings. There was something about Jessica that he failed to find in any other woman once the first flush of interest had faded.

'Oh, well! Do you drink vodka, Jess?' He grinned, offered her the brimming glass.

'No.' Her tone was uncompromising. He added insult to injury by offering her vodka, a drink he ought to know that she disliked, when he had left her with the promise of procuring the Cinzano that she did like—and forgotten all about her!

'I'll put it down somewhere. Want to dance, darling. You're looking a bit green about the gills. You haven't been sampling the punch, have you?'

She moved stiffly in his arms to the music, sensing that he held her with indifference and that his interest was centred on the pretty Irish nurse. It was foolish to be hurt. He was a little selfish, a little unthinking, but he did not mean to be cruel.

He was enjoying the party. Perhaps if she made an effort she could enjoy it, too. She knew many of the people who filled the house to overflowing. She had snubbed one of them quite mercilessly—and all because he had looked at her with a glow of admiration and she had no wish to become involved with any man but Clive. Which was probably very stupid and short-sighted because it was becoming increasingly obvious that her involvement with Clive was a dead end.

Jessica fought a foolish desire to burst into tears. She was tired after night duty. She was disappointed because she had looked forward to a very different kind of evening with Clive. She felt absurdly threatened by his interest in Amanda Flynn. She ought to be used to his weakness for a pretty face, the meaningless flirtations, the light-hearted affairs. He always came back to her and that was surely proof of a deep and lasting affection. One day he would settle down and be ready for marriage and she must be patient, she told herself, a little desperately ...

Later, they stood with friends in laughing conversation. With Clive still by her side and more attentive, Jessica could laugh at her fears and now the music did not seem so loud or a party seem such an unsatisfactory way to spend an evening with the man she loved.

Lester circulated. The party was a success. But it

would have been so without any effort on his part, he suspected. All this crowd needed was a venue, some music, plenty to drink and congenial company. At the moment, spirits were high and everyone was happy. No one had yet drunk too much or lost his girl to someone else or quarrelled with his best friend. Things were running smoothly.

He stood by the door, his gaze roving about the crowded room. His glance rested on one group, then another—and finally settled on a particular face. She was smiling at last, he noticed. Her expression was warm, laughing, vivid with life. She was very lovely. She stood with Clive Mortimer's arm around her slender waist, her gaze never leaving the man's face as he talked. Lester turned away abruptly.

A doctor in a busy teaching hospital came into contact with many attractive girls in the course of his work. Men like Clive Mortimer had been known to string along half a dozen at a time for young nurses seemed particularly impressed by good-looking doctors in white coats.

Lester had played the field, too. He was young, virile and he had a healthy interest in the opposite sex. But, like many men in his position, he had avoided the kind of involvement that led to marriage. As a medical student there had been little time or money for serious courtship but plenty of opportunities for light-hearted romance. Many doctors did marry nurses, of course. They had common ground on which to build a lasting relationship, a full understanding of the demands and difficulties of the profession, and they were thrown in each other's way all the time, on and off duty. So Hartlake, like any big teaching hospital, had its share of happiness and heartache among the staff.

Lester had never lost his heart to any of the girls in his life. But there was a promise of enchantment in the cool loveliness of a girl who seemed to have no time for him. He turned away, reminding himself that she was involved with Clive and obviously liked it that way. But it was not easy to shake off the persistent feeling that he was destined to love her . . .

While Jessica danced, Clive slipped away for a word with Amanda. She was very pretty, very appealing, and he was attracted. She was too young, of course. And it did not do for a senior doctor to pay too much attention to a very junior nurse. It was usually the girl who was hauled before Matron for a warning.

Fraternisation between the sexes was not approved but it could not be stamped out. One soon learned to be discreet and to conduct affairs outside the hospital walls. Amanda was much too pretty to ignore, Clive felt, and he had always found that it was worth taking the occasional risk.

She was sitting on the stairs, eyes sparkling, holding court. Flattered by his pursuit, she greeted him with a warmth he had anticipated and he squeezed into the narrow space by her side and set about persuading her to meet him on another evening.

Jessica was swept out into the hall and back again by her exuberant partner. In that brief moment, she saw Clive and Amanda Flynn with their heads together. It was only a glimpse but it was enough to send her heart plummeting with sudden despair.

Stifled by the heat, suddenly filled with a dislike of the people about her, Jessica slipped out of the house. The tiny garden was paved like a courtyard and was surprisingly secluded. Some of the revellers were in search of privacy and she tactfully avoided the dark corners with their meaningful murmurs, soft laughter, stirring shadows.

She went to the end of the garden and looked at the house, windows blazing with light. The sound of disco music shattered the night and she wondered what the neighbours thought of this noisy party.

The night air struck chill and Jessica shivered in her thin dress. Then, abruptly, she flared with anger. This was ridiculous! Why should she skulk in a strange garden because she could not bear to watch the slow destruction of her happiness, her hopes? She would find a telephone, ring for a taxi, leave Clive to do as he pleased with whom he pleased!

A man stepped from the shadows and she jumped, startled by the sudden movement. The light from the house fell on his face and she registered his identity without surprise or pleasure.

'Why don't you play him at his own game?' he said quietly. He had seen her hurried exit and guessed its cause. But she could not be unused to such treatment at Clive Mortimer's hands and he marvelled that she was prepared to suffer it without obvious protest. It implied that she was very much in love with the man.

'What!' She was angry rather than startled, disliking his obvious awareness of her discomfiture.

'It isn't my business,' Lester said gently. 'But you're a very lovely girl. Hasn't he looked at you lately? He certainly doesn't seem to value you.'

'It isn't your business,' she agreed icily, instantly contemptuous of such a hackneyed approach. She moved to pass him, to re-enter the house. He put out a hand and caught her wrist, not hurting, a light but decisive clasp that kept her by his side. His trained fingers caught the swift quickening of her pulse. She

30

looked at him and then at the encircling fingers, eyes widening, body stiff with indignation. 'Do you mind . . .!'

'I'm not going to leap on you,' he said, a smile lurking behind the words. 'Despite temptation . . .' Her eyes flashed with fury. 'I just want to talk to you.'

'We've nothing to say to each other!'

'How do you know?' he returned reasonably. 'This could be the beginning of a beautiful friendship.'

Jessica struggled to free herself. 'I doubt it!'

'We have something very important in common— and that must be an excellent start.'

She stared at him. 'What are you talking about?' she demanded impatiently. 'What could we possibly have in common?'

'Your happiness.'

A little shock rippled down Jessica's spine. Uttered by a man who was little more than a stranger, the words were amazing, alarming—and oddly moving. Taken by surprise, she ceased the struggle to free her wrist. She stared at him doubtfully. 'My happiness . . .' she echoed in astonishment. 'Why should that concern you?'

'I don't know,' he said with truth, with a hint of wry humour. 'I don't know you or very much about you. But your happiness means a great deal to me, I find. Would you like me to punch Clive's nose for him?'

She moved impatiently. 'You're drunk!'

Lester dropped his hand from her wrist. He regarded her steadily, a faint smile curving his mouth. 'That would be a more acceptable explanation, I daresay. It must be embarrassing to be told by a virtual stranger that he's in love with you.'

Jessica caught her breath. 'Don't be absurd!'

'It is absurd,' he agreed. 'That's what I keep telling myself. "Some enchanted evening . . . across a crowded room . . ." I've never believed in it, much. Love at first sight belongs in romantic novels. Don't you agree? Anyway, it isn't love at first sight. I've seen you many times in various places even if you don't remember me. I think I've always known that you were meant to be really important and tonight I knew why!'

'I'm cold,' Jessica said, rather desperately. It seemed heartless to desert a man in the middle of a declaration of love. But he was almost a stranger—and he was either mad or drunk or both!

'Don't go,' he said swiftly, urgently. 'Not yet!' He stripped off his denim jacket and draped it about her shoulders with gentle hands. She stood irresolute, knowing she should leave him but sufficiently feminine to wonder what next he would find to say to her! 'I've had a drink or two, of course—enough to cast off inhibition and loosen my tongue, perhaps. Or I might not be saying these things to you. But I mean every word!'

'Well, it doesn't do you a scrap of good,' she said bluntly, knowing she must be cruel to be kind in the end. 'I don't know a thing about you. I don't even like you!'

'Feminine logic,' he said wryly. 'Not knowing me, how can you be so sure that you don't like me? Give a man a fair chance, sweetheart!' He smiled at her with warm and tender amusement.

'There isn't any point . . .'

'There is for me. I want to marry you.'

Jessica was shaken by the quiet resolution, the air of utter certainty. Against her will, she was impressed.

'That isn't possible,' she said, more kindly.

'Impossible things happen all the time,' he said with conviction.

'Not in my life,' she told him firmly.

He searched her uncompromising eyes for a moment. Then, surprising himself as much as her, he bent his head and kissed her with an almost reverent tenderness. Jessica's hands flew to his chest. But she had no need to keep him at bay. There was nothing to alarm her in that kiss which seemed to give so much and ask nothing in return. He raised his head and captured her hands for the merest of moments in both his own. Then he stooped to retrieve the coat that had slipped from her shoulders.

Jessica left him abruptly, thrusting her way into the house, snatching at the first familiar person to protect her from the disturbing attentions of a stranger who kissed her like a lover . . .

CHAPTER THREE

CLIVE moved across the room to Jessica. He put his arms about her waist, nuzzling the nape of her slender neck with his lips. She stiffened, resisting, furious. Turning swiftly, she relaxed, relieved.

'Where were you?' he murmured.

Words and tone implied that he had missed her, hunted high and low to find her. And perhaps he had, she thought, giving him the benefit of the doubt. She must not make too much of his interest in another girl at a party where everyone was flirting.

'Out in the garden. I needed some fresh air.' She

discovered that she was slightly on the defensive. As if it mattered that he might have seen or someone had said that she was in the shadows of the secluded garden with another man. It had been an innocent encounter as far as she was concerned. It was not her fault that she had attracted the attention of an eccentric young man!

In any case, Clive was not jealous or at all possessive. Probably because he did not care enough, she thought wryly. Sometimes he seemed almost too anxious to push her into the arms of other men—usually when he was in hot pursuit of a new conquest!

'Everything all right, darling?' Clive gave her an affectionate hug, feeling a twinge of conscience. Amanda Flynn was a bewitching creature and he could not resist the teasing promise in her green eyes. But he was very fond of Jessica. She was a grand girl who made no demands and offered no reproaches and that could be said of very few women!

He valued her affection and friendship even if it did seem that he took them for granted. They had a special relationship that was like no other in his life. He liked women too much to settle down with just one but Jessica was something special and the bond between them survived for reasons that he did not bother to analyse.

Jessica looked up at him with a faint plea in her grey eyes. 'Sorry—but I'd like to go home. I've had enough, Clive.'

He raised an eyebrow. 'So soon?'

'Please.' Out of the corner of her eye, she could see her *bête noire*. He seemed perfectly normal but she knew better! He had glanced her way once or twice and she had avoided meeting his eyes, knowing it

34

would be foolish to show the slightest encouragement. She suspected that he was only waiting for the right moment to approach her again.

'All right, darling. If you say so.' Clive was enjoying the party but no doubt Jessica was tired from night duty. She was not her usual bright and cheerful self, certainly. Perhaps the party had been a mistake. But he had been glad of the chance to further a fleeting acquaintance with the Irish girl. However, it was Jessica's evening, the first they had spent together for some time. He had missed her, he suddenly realised. He smiled at her, his eyes warm. 'I can think of better ways to spend the rest of the evening, anyway,' he said softly, meaningfully. She smiled, a little doubtfully—and Clive laughed, confident that there would be no doubt in her eyes or in her response when he took her into his arms. 'But we'd better have a word with our host even if it's only hello and goodbye!'

Jessica wondered which of the many people was their host. It was such a haphazard party that it might be any one of them. Lester Thorn, whoever he was, must be a very good-natured, easy-going and popular person!

With a hand about her waist, Clive guided her through the press of people. Too late, she realised that they were heading for the one man she had no desire to meet again.

'Fantastic party!' Clive laid a hand on his friend's shoulder. Lester turned with his ready, warm smile. 'We've had a terrific time, haven't we, Jess?'

'You aren't going yet, I hope. The night is young.' He spoke to Clive but glanced involuntarily at his companion. Their eyes met and his smile deepened.

35

Jessica found that his eyes were a very deep blue, very striking, and she wondered that she had failed to notice them when they met on the ward or talked earlier in the evening. Perhaps she had not really looked at him until now. He was attractive if one liked the type. She did not, she decided firmly.

'Must, old man,' Clive said lightly, brightly. 'We've a wedding in the morning and can't afford to lose too much sleep.'

'Not your wedding, I imagine?' His tone was very dry.

Clive grinned. 'You must be joking! Marriage and medicine don't mix!'

'Well, it was good of you to come ... both of you,' he said with another glance at the lovely face with its polite and meaningless smile. There was just a hint of betraying colour in her oval face, just a spark of challenge in the wide grey eyes. Otherwise she could have been just another friend of a friend waiting to shake hands with a stranger and thank him for a lovely evening.

'But you two don't know each other, do you?' Clive abruptly recalled. 'I can't think why not! However ... Jessica Brook, would-be matron! Lester Thorn, would-be consultant surgeon!'

Lester ignored the flippancy. 'But we do know each other,' he said gently, warmly, speaking directly to Jessica. She looked at him in swift and defiant repudiation and he smiled with warm understanding.

'We've met,' she said tartly. 'Very briefly. One doctor is just like another when I'm busy on a ward.'

Clive was startled. She was usually a warm and friendly girl. He had expected her to respond to the unmistakable interest in his friend's attitude. Instead, she had slapped him down with a vengeance. Maybe she had her reasons but it was a little embarrassing. He said hastily: 'That's why it's good to meet socially, don't you think? Break down some of the barriers. Most of them are hangovers from the Stone Age, anyway. It's ridiculous that we almost expect to be shot at dawn if we take time off to chat up a pretty nurse occasionally.'

'Very true,' Lester agreed lightly, amused. 'I hope that one or two barriers went down this evening.' The words were meaningful. Jessica resolutely refused to meet his smiling eyes. 'The doctor–nurse relationship can only benefit from a closer understanding. Don't you agree, Jessica?'

She would not thaw despite the gentle warmth of his teasing. She was incensed that her name on his lips sounded more like an endearment. Did he want the whole world to suppose that they were indulging in a secret affair? He looked and spoke like a lover—and surely Clive could not be blind and deaf to all the implications?

'Certainly—if the patients also benefit,' she said coldly. 'But too many juniors spend too much time chatting and flirting with medical students and house-men when there's a great deal of work to be done on the ward. If that's what you mean by a closer under-standing, as I suspect, then I fail to see how it can benefit the patients. Some barriers must still be main-tained, in my opinion.'

Clive laughed and drew her to him with an arm about her slim shoulders. 'Another Sister Booth in the making,' he declared lightly, referring to an elderly dragon of a ward sister, now retired, whose rigid dis-cipline and sharp tongue still lived on in the memories of those nurses and medical students who had once incurred her wrath. Sister Booth had run her ward for many years with a rod of iron and even the crustiest of consultants had occasionally bowed to her superior judgment and long experience.

Jessica smiled wryly. She was strict with juniors and it did not always make for popularity. But patients must come first, no matter what, and it was often vital that a nurse obeyed an instruction without hesitation or question. At the same time, she did not encourage blind obedience as it was often very necessary for a nurse to use her own initiative.

She did not mind the comparison with Sister Booth where her work was concerned. But that tyrant had been heartily disliked if respected by her colleagues. At the same time, she had been much loved by the patients in her care. It hurt to recall that the patients had been Sister Booth's children, her only family, her sole interest in life. Was that to be Jessica's fate? Never to know the joy and satisfaction of husband, home and children. There were times when it seemed only too likely!

'The first-years call me Bossy Boots,' she admitted lightly. 'I expect the cap fits but I often wish they could have a taste of Sister Booth. We might have walked in fear and trembling but she knew how to inspire respect—and she could certainly teach!'

'The old order changeth,' Clive said airily, abruptly bored. 'Come along, darling. Say goodnight to the nice man and let's be on our way. It's late.'

Reluctantly, Jessica held out her hand to Lester Thorn. 'Well, goodnight. It was . . . quite a party,' she said carefully.

His hand closed over her slender fingers. 'Memorable, anyway,' he said, smiling. He bent his dark head to kiss her on the cheek. 'I'm very glad you came, Jessica.'

She was annoyed. He had no right to kiss her with the privileged ease of friendship and no right to smile at her in just that way, she thought crossly, not so much embarrassed as shaken by the warm tenderness in the deep blue eyes. She did not want to remember the way he had kissed her in the garden or recall the things he had said with so little reason and not the slightest encouragement.

Clive was quiet as they walked along the narrow street to his parked car. Jessica slipped her hand into his arm. To him, it seemed a gesture of reassurance.

He glanced down at her. 'I thought you didn't know Thorn,' he said. He was not jealous. He was not in love with Jessica nor did he feel that he had any particular claim on her affections. But he did dislike deceit of any kind.

'I don't,' she said firmly.

'He kissed you.'

'Oh, darling! He was probably drunk!' she declared gaily. 'Anyway, everyone kisses everyone else at parties ... don't they?' she added with light but quite unmistakable meaning.

Clive suddenly laughed. 'Oh, you saw that, did you?' He squeezed the hand that rested on his arm. 'She's a pretty kid and she was giving them away. Am I the man to refuse a free kiss?' He took his car keys from his pocket and opened the passenger door. 'As you say, it doesn't mean a thing.'

Jessica believed him. Clive was a man who took what the gods offered with laughing delight. He took his work seriously but the rest of life was little more than an enjoyable whirl to him, she often thought. He had so much going for him ... looks, charm, personality and more money than he knew what to do with thanks to a legacy from a doting grandmother.

He could snatch a kiss from a stranger at a party and never give the girl another thought. And why not? It was a healthy, wholesome attitude and more easily understood than that of a man who talked of loving and was too intense for comfort. Jessica wished she could put Lester Thorn out of her mind and wondered why it was not the simplest thing in the world to do so. But his attractive, lean face, the slightly crooked smile and those very blue eyes seemed to be vividly etched on her mind's eye ...

The roads were quiet. Clive drove with one hand on the steering wheel, the other covering Jessica's loosely linked fingers as they lay in her lap. He was feeling euphoric. It had been a good evening and the best was yet to come, he thought confidently. Jessica had been keeping him at a distance of late but he sensed that she was in a relaxed, melting mood and glad to be with him this evening. He turned to smile at her and desire quickened at the thought of her in his arms.

For him, there had been a succession of women. But not one quite like Jessica who was so sweet, so warmly generous in her response—and utterly lacking in the irritating possessiveness that he had found in other girls. Jessica did not expect a proposal of marriage whenever he made love to her, he thought thankfully. Perhaps that was one of the reasons why he would eventually marry her ...

Jessica opened the door of the flat and slipped the key back into her purse. 'I'll make coffee,' she said. 'Then I'm sending you home.'

'Darling, that's the third time you've warned me off,' he said in light reproach. 'Don't you love me any more?'

He followed her into the tiny kitchen and watched as she filled the kettle, took a jar of instant coffee from a cupboard and set two mugs on a tray. It seemed to him that she had something on her mind.

'Seriously, Jess . . .' He was suddenly sober. For some reason, he recalled the way that Thorn had kissed her, the way that Thorn had looked at her—and he knew the oddest conviction that she had not been surprised or dismayed. Yet she continued to deny that she knew the man. He reached for her hands and pulled her to him. 'We've known each other a long time,' he said quietly, searching the wide grey eyes. 'You'd tell me if there was someone else?'

She leaned against him, surprised but pleased by the sudden concern. 'Do you always tell me?' she teased gently, woman-like.

He put his arms about her and held her close, pressing his cheek to the soft fair hair. 'No one else matters and you know it! You're my girl,' he said warmly.

Jessica stifled a sigh. The glib words were all too familiar but she had to believe that he meant them. He had been an important part of her life for a very long time.

He kissed her and she allowed him to hold her, briefly. Then she drew away, smiling to soften the rebuff. In the past she had given too freely, she thought wryly. Perhaps he would value her more if she kept him at arms' length. Perhaps he would merely turn to girls like Amanda Flynn. It was a chance she would just have to take!

'Coffee,' she said firmly, moving to switch off the boiling kettle.

'First . . .?' His eyes danced with mischief, light-hearted confidence.

'Instead!'

He laughed softly. But he was a little shaken by that note of resolution. She was not a tease and it had always warmed and delighted him that she welcomed and returned his kisses, his lovemaking, with love and understanding. Did she really mean to end their easy and comfortable intimacy? It was a disturbing thought.

They had been occasional, light-hearted lovers since he had taken an eighteen-year-old virgin by storm with his engaging smile and smooth-talking charm. She had fallen in love with him. He had been unable to disregard his growing affection and lasting need of her but considered himself incapable of the kind of loving that a woman seemed to expect from a man. Their undemanding relationship suited him very well and he wanted it to continue.

They carried their coffees into the sitting-room. Side by side on the sofa, they talked of impersonal things and he did not attempt to kiss her or touch her again. Jessica was relieved. She was also puzzled by her lack of feeling. Was she still smarting over his unmistakable interest in Amanda Flynn? Knowing him, she did not usually take it so much to heart whenever he briefly fancied another girl.

Throughout the years, her love for Clive had remained constant against all odds. She had accepted his short-lived infatuations with other girls and, despite well-meant advice from friends, she had refrained from retaliating with flirtations of her own. She had never been tempted. Loving Clive, she only wanted

42

him. Loving Clive, she could forgive and forget, open her arms to him when he came back, accept when he strayed once more and continue to hope that he would eventually realise she was the most important woman in his life. At the same time, she had managed not to parade the way she felt about him so that he did not have to feel guilty about his flirtations and he obviously believed that she was content with their on-off relationship.

Now, suddenly, she was impatient with him for taking her so much for granted. Perhaps she was tiring of always being available whenever he chose to turn to her. Even her patience might be wearing thin after so long, she thought wryly. Or was it only that it was spring and weddings were in the air and she felt oddly threatened by Amanda Flynn although it was unlikely that the girl would hold Clive's fickle interest for very long.

Clive drained his coffee and rose. 'We're making an early start in the morning. I'd better let you get to bed,' he said lightly. 'I'll call for you at eight-thirty.'

'You're going . . .?' Now, perversely, she was disappointed. He had been so easily deterred from lovemaking that now she wondered if he had wanted her at all!

'Isn't that what you want, my sweet?'

The diffidence in his manner caught at her heart. Had she hurt him? He never seemed to be particularly vulnerable but perhaps he was clever at concealing his feelings. Even she might not know him as well as she believed.

She held out her hand to him impulsively. 'I want you to be happy,' she said, meaning it. 'I love you . . .'

Later, lying beside him, Jessica felt an unaccount-

43

able depression. How could it be wrong to go to bed with the man she loved? Yet why did she feel that she had betrayed something deep within herself?

He had made love to her with an ardour that ought to have dispelled all her doubts, all the hurt of the early evening. She had responded as he expected but much of it had been pretence and she hoped that he had been deceived. She had been puzzled by that lack of response to his kiss, his caress, his eager passion. It had always pleased her to give, to content him, to forge another link in their relationship. She had always cherished the precious moments of intimacy when it seemed that he might love her for all his insistence on freedom and independence.

He was half-asleep, his arm thrown carelessly across her body. She studied the handsome features, noted the faint smile of satisfaction that curved the mobile mouth, thought for the thousandth time that no man ought to be quite so good-looking!

Abruptly she realised that she was studying him dispassionately. Always in the past, she had looked on him with loving eyes that blinded her to the weakness and selfishness in that handsome face. Now, with a shock of dismay, she found herself wondering why she loved him so much—and wasn't that only one step away from wondering if she loved him at all!

Hastily she thrust away such treacherous thoughts. She could not imagine what her life would be like if she did not have Clive to love and the hope of marrying him one day to sustain her through the demanding and sometimes difficult work of a staff nurse in a busy hospital.

She snuggled close to him and touched her lips to his cheek. He smiled drowsily and murmured her

44

name before drifting deeper into sleep. A wealth of tender affection engulfed her so promptly that she relaxed into the comfortable belief of loving that had become more of a habit than she knew . . .

The sky was grey for the wedding but it didn't rain. And Suzy's smile lit up the day so that no one noticed the absence of the sun. Every bride is beautiful but it seemed to Jessica that her friend glowed with a special beauty. She was envious. For Suzy's radiance could only be born of a loving that knew it was returned in full measure.

She stole a glance at Clive, standing beside her in the pew, tall and handsome in formal clothes. Her heart quickened in instant admiration of his good looks, his air of assurance. He was a distinguished man. Born to go far, she often thought, for he was good at his job and would undoubtedly become a consultant in the not-too-distant future. It would be nice to be sure that she would share that future with him, she thought wistfully . . .

Clive sensed her thoughts and stiffened his resolution. He disliked weddings and too many of their friends were taking the plunge just lately. He felt it was making Jessica feel restless and dissatisfied. He knew that she wanted to marry him and there were moments when he toyed with the idea—last night, for instance, in the afterglow of lovemaking. But it was an impulse he had no real difficulty in suppressing.

Jessica would make an ideal wife for a successful consultant and when he came close to attaining that ambition, he would ask her to marry him. He did not doubt that she would wait. In the meantime, she had her own career and was obviously destined to be a ward sister in the near future. In old-fashioned terms, they had an understanding. It had worked well enough for the Victorians and it worked very well for them. He was not tied down which mattered to him and Jessica was equally free to have other men-friends if she wished . . .

The reception was crowded for Suzy had always been popular and it seemed that every off-duty member of the hospital staff had come along to drink a toast to her happiness with her new husband.

'Weddings are in fashion this year!'

'Your turn next, Jessica!'

'Isn't it time that you two named the day?'

Clive took the teasing in good part. It was inevitable, he realised. They had been regarded as a couple by too many people for too long.

And Suzy, giving him a special smile when he kissed the bride, said softly: 'I shall miss my Jess. Look after her for me, Clive . . . make her happy.'

'Yes, of course,' he promised, knowing what she meant. Newly-weds were always so anxious to have their friends follow the example that they had set. But he felt a stirring of resentment that it was taken so much for granted that Jessica's happiness lay with him. It could be a handicap to a man if he was rumoured to be virtually engaged, he thought with a hint of impatience.

'Poor darling . . .' Jessica squeezed his arm sympathetically. 'You're looking trapped.' She was teasing but she smiled warmly, with understanding. 'People get these ideas into their heads and nothing will shake them out.'

He looked down at her, a faint frown in his blue eyes. 'You don't want to get married, do you, Jess?'

There was only one answer to such a loaded question, of course. 'No, darling,' she said soothingly, amused. It was ironic that it was the nearest he had ever come to a proposal, she thought dryly.

'That's my girl!' He put an arm about her shoulders and hugged her to him. 'The mere thought of it gives me the horrors!'

Jessica realised that he was in earnest. All day, tears had been just below the surface for weddings are emotional affairs for any woman. Now they welled and she bit her lip fiercely to keep them back. Damn him! She had loved him for six years and he had been stringing her along with the hint of marriage as the carrot! But he would never marry her, come what may! Clive was just not the marrying kind . . . or was it only that she was not the kind of girl that a man like Clive wished to marry? It would be just the kind of cruel joke that life liked to play if he was to fall headlong in love with someone else and be married within a month, she thought with sudden bitterness.

Six years of loving—and all for nothing. He still cared so little that the prospect of marrying her filled him with horror. What a poor creature she must be to trail along at his heels, completely lacking in pride, swallowing every humiliation . . . and all in the name of love!

It was time that she pulled herself together and stopped making such a fool of herself over a man who really did not want her. It was time that she proved to Clive and to everyone else at Hartlake that he was not the only pebble on the beach.

It was a pity that there was something about Lester Thorn that she could not like. Or he might have been the ideal person to show the world how little she really cared about Clive . . .

CHAPTER FOUR

IT was a warm day and Lester took advantage of the sunshine to spend part of his lunch break in the large square garden that was surrounded on all sides by the hospital buildings and dominated by the imposing statue of Henry Hartlake, founder of the hospital.

It was a pleasant and popular spot on a spring day, much in use as a short cut from one part of the busy hospital to another, and he relaxed on one of the benches that ran around the base of the statue.

He glanced through a newspaper, exchanged a word or two with his neighbour, watched the antics of some medical students who were erecting rows of colourful bunting in readiness for Founder's Week that culminated in the highlight of the hospital year, Founder's Ball. Then he turned his attention to a group of junior nurses who had gathered on the grass to make the most of a brief pause in their busy day.

They were first-year nurses, very young and lively, quite charming in the traditional uniform that gave Hartlake nurses a much-valued distinction since the national uniform had been introduced into so many hospitals. As student nurses, they wore the blue check dresses of crisp cotton with short, puffed sleeves and matching belts and the tiny white caps with the one blue stripe of a first-year nurse. Watching them, heads bent studiously over textbooks and apparently testing each other on various questions, he guessed that they were P.T.S. nurses preparing for Sister Tutor's examination before beginning practical work on the wards.

It was a pretty scene. Lester had observed it many times, of course. But it always gave him pleasure. He felt a tremendous pride in being associated with a famous teaching hospital like Hartlake. Hartlake nurses, like those of Guy's and Thomas's and Bart's, were known and sought after throughout the world.

There was much toing and froing through the garden. Lester glanced idly at the people who passed by. Nurses, doctors, students, porters, patients and their relatives and friends, physiotherapists, social workers and a variety of ancillary staff. Some faces were familiar. Occasionally he smiled and acknowledged a greeting. There was such an air of purpose about most of those who used the garden as a short cut that few glanced his way.

The tall, slender girl in the blue striped dress and the fluted cap of a staff nurse did not look at anyone as she walked briskly along the paved path, cloak swinging from her shoulders, arms folded across her breasts in the traditional manner of nurses.

Lester rose, his heart thudding, his lips suddenly dry as he knew again that swift certainty of caring. He had not seen her since the night that Clive Mortimer had brought her to his party but she had been constantly in his thoughts.

She did not appear to notice him. As she reached him, he fell into step by her side. 'Jessica . . .' he said, her name both a greeting and an endearment.

She glanced at him impatiently. She was out of sympathy with all men just now and she wanted nothing to do with a man whose very blue eyes shone with such a fanatical light of love without the least encouragement.

She was not sure that she could cope with such intensity of emotion. And he was not the man that she wanted to love her, she thought with a familiar surge of sadness.

'I'm in a hurry,' she said coldly.

'I'm going your way,' he returned cheerfully.

Deliberately she quickened her pace. She was a little late, as it happened. She also wished to escape from him.

'Fire or haemorrhage, nurse,' he murmured, teasing her gently, as she whisked through the swing doors that he opened for her. Her skirts rustled as she hurried along the corridor to the lifts.

Several people were waiting for the lift and she managed to lose him in the crowd. Resolutely she kept her gaze from wandering towards him although she was aware that he had followed her into the lift. By the second floor there was only herself and Lester Thorn in the lift as it moved upwards once more.

'Where are you working?' he asked with a very natural interest.

'Paterson.'

He nodded. 'How do you get on with Ruth Challis?'

'Fine, thanks.' She did not mean to encourage any lengthy conversation and she was glad as the doors slid open. She stepped out into the corridor. Lester followed. At the swing doors of the ward, she turned to him with a hint of impatience. 'Have you business on Paterson?'

'Not at the moment.' He glanced at his watch 'I'm still off duty, as it happens.'

'Then what do you want?' she demanded crossly.

'You,' he said promptly, with truth.

'Oh, for heaven's sake . . .!' She turned away.

Lester detained her with a light but determined touch on her arm. 'All right, Jessica. We'll play it the conventional way,' he said, reassuring her.

'It isn't a game!' Her tone was tart.

'No, it isn't,' he agreed quietly. 'This is for real—and for life.'

She bit her lip. She had walked into that, she thought wryly. Her heart quickened with a hint of anxiety. There was something disturbing about this man and his insistence that she was his destiny.

'I wish you'd take no for an answer,' she said, a little desperately.

'But you must see how impossible that is for me,' he returned reasonably. 'I love you, Jessica.'

Her heart jumped at the calm and oddly convincing statement. She looked away from those smiling eyes, irritated that anyone could be fool enough to fall in love with a stranger—and yet uncomfortably aware that Lester Thorn was nobody's fool.

'Well, I'm sorry,' she said flatly. 'But I can't help that. You'll just have to get over it as best you can. Just leave me alone. I won't be hounded like this by someone I don't even want to know!'

She pushed through the swing doors of the ward. She hung up her cloak and pinned on the clean white apron that was the symbol of being on duty. She was annoyed to find that her hands were shaking slightly. She prided herself on her coolness. Maybe her dislike of Lester Thorn stemmed from the fact that he flustered her, made her feel unsure of herself. She refused to think of the look in his eyes as she broke away from him, the sudden throb of a nerve in his lean cheek, the visible change of colour that might have been due to shock or pain or anger. He had no right to pursue her to the very doors of the ward. He had no right to waylay her in the first place. He had no right to imagine himself in love with a woman he did not even know!

She joined the group of nurses who had gathered about the desk for the reading of the report. 'Sorry I'm late, Sister,' she said automatically, taking a pen from her pocket in readiness for the notes she would need to make.

Ruth Challis looked at her curiously. The girl was flushed and seemed a little upset and the grey eyes seemed almost too large in that lovely oval face. There was a rumour that Clive Mortimer was paying a great deal of attention to the pretty Irish nurse on Currie. And Ruth knew, in common with many others at Hartlake, that Jessica Brook had been carrying the torch for Clive Mortimer ever since her early student days. He was a shocking flirt and everyone knew it but that did not seem to deter the girls who fell for his looks and charm—and it did not seem to deter Jessica Brook from caring for him. Women were the oddest creatures!

She did not know Jessica well but she liked her and she felt sorry for her. She was an excellent nurse and it was too bad of Clive Mortimer or any other man to make a mess of her personal life, she thought with compassion, having known heartache for herself in the past. She wondered if Jessica was particularly worried about this latest affair. It seemed to be more serious than usual. Certainly the couple were not being very discreet. The girl was ridiculously young but he ought to know better than to make her the subject of so much gossip.

Report finished, she sent Jessica to give a patient a

pre-med. Paterson was a surgical ward and there was much to be done and it would be as well if the girl was kept too busy to brood.

Mrs Weston was a boisterous, cheerful woman who was about to have a hysterectomy. She had six sons and she was glad of the rest, she told Jessica. She was relaxed and untroubled by thoughts of the operation.

'Can't be worse than childbirth, gel,' she said comfortably. 'Not one of my boys weighed less than eight pounds and all of them bloody lazy. Hard work then and hard work now. Keep you poor and break your heart—that's kids! Take my word for it!' The loving pride in eyes and voice belied the words.

Jessica smiled at her warmly. 'I think you're a very lucky woman, Mrs Weston.'

'I'd have liked a girl,' she said wistfully. 'Kept trying, we did. My last was a girl. Lost her at five months. Tripped over my Michael's skate and fell down the bloody stairs. That's what did the damage, see. I've never been really right since.'

'You'll be fine when you come back to the ward. Mr Eaton is one of our best surgeons.'

'A lovely man, isn't he? Tall, dark and handsome— just my type. Lovely manners, too. I bet all you nurses fancy him. Going to put me to sleep with that thing, are you?' she demanded, a wary eye on the hypodermic in Jessica's hand.

'This is just to relax you, Mrs Weston. You'll go along to Theatres very soon and then you'll have another injection—and when you wake up it will be all over. There's nothing to worry about . . .'

She set up a drip for a patient who had just come back from Theatres and then took round the drugs trolley with a third-year nurse to check each dose in case of error. It took a long time because it was an opportunity to get to know the patients, to talk to them and find out how they felt and if they had any anxieties or problems.

On a very busy ward, such as Paterson, a nurse had little time to get to know the patients and there were sure to be admissions and discharges during her off-duty. Each patient assumed that every doctor and nurse who came into the ward was familiar with the details of his or her case. So it was important to pay special attention to Sister's report when coming on-duty and to make that swift, comprehensive study of the patient's chart and to remember the notes scribbled hastily in one's notebook or, sometimes, on the underside of one's starched apron.

Jessica was a good nurse who loved her work and she had the happy knack of establishing cheerful rapport with a patient in just a few words. She was warmhearted, genuinely interested in people, and she enjoyed every aspect of nursing. It was just as well that she found it so satisfying, she thought a little wryly, thinking of Clive while she smiled and chatted and dispensed reassurance along with tablets and medicines. For it was possible that nursing would prove to be her lifelong career.

She had decided that it must be the parting of the ways for her and Clive. She loved him still and old habits died hard but she knew that she would never find real happiness with him. He did not and never would love her as she wanted and needed to be loved. He took life and love too lightly, reserving his real dedication for his work and ambition.

Jessica did not want him to marry her because she would be a suitable wife or because he felt that he

54

owed her marriage in return for the love and loyalty of years. She was much too proud. And one day she might meet a man she could trust as well as love who would wish to marry her for the right reasons.

Instead of spending the rest of her off-duty days with Clive as he had expected, she had driven down to Berkshire to visit the tactful and understanding aunt who had brought her up after the loss of her parents in a flying accident. Jessica had desperately felt the need of a breathing space. She had returned with her mind made up and it had been no surprise to find that Clive had been busy with Amanda Flynn in her absence. The discovery had strengthened her resolve to break with him. It was almost unfortunate that it did not tempt her to take advantage of Lester Thorn's convenient admiration. But even for the sake of her pride she did not feel that she could make use of a man that she did not like.

Ruth Challis went to tea, leaving Jessica in charge of the ward as the most senior nurse on duty that afternoon. Mrs Weston was back from Theatres and in a side ward. Jessica was making her comfortable when a junior nurse put her head into the room and announced in a voice of doom that Professor Wilmot had arrived to do a late round.

Jessica almost groaned. The consultant was a most difficult man, rude and sarcastic with the nursing staff, brusque with patients who were often too awed to make intelligent answers to barked questions, and very impatient with students who sometimes appeared ignorant because he intimidated them. Ward staff disliked him and dreaded his rounds that often took place at very inconvenient and disruptive times. But he was a very brilliant man, internationally known for his

55

sometimes controversial research into open heart surgery. He lacked the bedside manner but perhaps he just did not like the teaching that was a necessary part of his consultancy at Hartlake, Jessica thought charitably, as she hurried to join the group who had already gathered about the patient's bed.

Someone stepped aside to allow her access to the patient's chart which she hastily took from the rail and handed to the Professor. He glanced at her with a scowl. 'Good of you to join us, nurse,' he said with heavy irony.

He glanced at the chart and then turned to the patient, a middle-aged woman who needed a heart valve replacement. He asked one or two questions and then began to detail the patient's history, her symptoms and the operation he intended to perform on the following day. The students listened attentively for he was apt to bark a question without warning.

Most consultants who only wished to lecture a group of students on a particular patient usually told the attendant nurse that she might continue with her work. In such circumstances, her presence was a convention rather than a necessity. Jessica fumed beneath her dutiful demeanour, thinking of the hundred and one things she could be doing.

Out of the corner of her eye, she saw Ruth Challis return to the ward, accompanied by Lester Thorn. The ward sister looked surprisingly youthful, even pretty, as she smiled and talked to the Registrar. For the first time, Jessica saw him as a man who was probably very attractive to women. Tall and lean with crisply waving dark hair and deep-set, very blue eyes, she could not deny that the slow, warm smile lightened his entire face and probably quickened the heartbeats of the susceptible. Recalling the confidence of his approach, she did not doubt that he was fully aware of his appeal to her sex. She did not like him but she had to admit that he was impressive.

Ruth sent her a glance of warm understanding and sat down at the desk to deal with some paper-work. Lester came to join the group of students about the patient's bed. Jessica had forgotten that he was a member of the Professor's team and she wondered how he got on with the crusty old curmudgeon.

She met his eyes—and he looked away. It was ridiculous to feel rebuffed, she told herself sternly. She had brushed him off in no uncertain manner and she could not expect him to behave as though it had never happened. What did she want, anyway? Certainly not Lester Thorn! There was a ruthlessness about him that was frightening, she felt. He was too direct, too sure of what he wanted—and in the habit of getting it, she fancied!

She was careful not to look at him again. Very soon, the Professor thrust the chart at her with a curt, 'Thank you, nurse ... I'm obliged to you!' His tone left her in no doubt that he had been fully aware of her restless impatience throughout his lecture.

He marched off with his gaggle of students in tow. Jessica bent over the patient, taking her hand and talking to her quietly, reassuringly, for she had been rather upset by the consultant's manner.

Suddenly she was aware that Lester Thorn was waiting patiently at the foot of the bed. Dutifully she drew back.

'Just a few words, Miss Ives,' he said gently, with his warm smile. 'I know you're very tired. But I also know that you are feeling anxious.' He drew a chair

57

close to the bed and sat down. 'Why don't you ask me anything that puzzles or worries you and I'll try to set your mind at rest. Clinical discussions can be very alarming, I'm afraid. Put into layman's language nothing is so very bad, believe me.'

Jessica left him to talk to the patient, wondering why she was forever falling over a man whose existence she had scarcely realised until recently. Or had she seen and spoken to him countless times, even worked with him, and never registered him as anything but just another doctor among the many at Hartlake? He had claimed to know her. She could not remember having met him until that night on Currie when she had lost a patient so unexpectedly.

It was not unusual for a big teaching hospital, of course. People could work side by side for months, not really knowing anything about each other, never meeting off the wards, friendly but impersonal. A nurse's uniform was a cloak of anonymity, Jessica thought wryly, recalling how often she had met ex-patients or even colleagues outside the hospital precincts who had failed to recognise her out of uniform. Patients often reproached a nurse for not complying with a request that they had made of an entirely different nurse. Jessica was used to it, now. In the early days of her training, it had been disconcerting to realise that all nurses look alike to many patients—and sometimes to her fellow-staff, too. To some extent, a doctor's white coat also made him just as faceless and nameless in many cases.

Lester Thorn stayed with Miss Ives for some time. Going about her work on the ward, Jessica could not help but be aware of him. Unbidden, the word *gentle* came to mind. For all his air of purpose, his obviously forceful character and that infuriating arrogance, he was a man who cared about people, she felt. He seemed to know just the right thing to say to the patients and his manner was neither too casual, too condescending or too professional.

On his way from the ward, he paused briefly at the desk to speak to Ruth Challis. Helping a junior to make up a bed for a new admission, Jessica noticed that they seemed to be on very friendly terms. Perhaps they knew each other well. She had never heard a word of gossip about the ward sister who was rumoured to be so dedicated to her work that she had no time for romance. Jessica did not believe that a woman existed who could not find time to fall in love if the right man came along . . . and Ruth Challis had never looked so pretty as she did at that moment, talking to the attractive Registrar.

As she neared the desk with her arms full of linen, Lester said lightly to Ruth: 'Just after ten in the Kingfisher, then. I'll look forward to it.' He turned and almost collided with Jessica.

He murmured an apology so perfunctory as to be painful and did not even look at her as he went on his way. She doubted if he even realised which nurse had bumped into him. His mind was obviously on the date he had just arranged with Ruth Challis. Well, good luck to them both, Jessica thought, with an odd little touch of defiance. She only hoped it was not a stupid attempt to make her regret turning him down for she liked Ruth and would not wish her to be used in such a fashion . . .

The evening was so busy that she had no time to think about him again. They had two emergency admissions, teenage sisters hurt in a car accident. One was badly injured and went to Theatres for immediate surgery. The younger girl had leg and head injuries and would probably need plastic surgery.

Due to go off duty at ten, it was nearer half past when Jessica and Ruth Challis left the ward together. The older woman glanced at her watch. 'I did have a date,' she said ruefully.

'I expect he's still waiting,' Jessica said lightly. 'He seems the reliable type.' She fancied it was true. Anyway, Lester Thorn would know and understand the circumstances that sometimes kept a nurse on the ward past her duty hours. 'You are meeting Lester Thorn, aren't you?'

Ruth glanced at her curiously. 'Yes, I am. Do you know him well?'

'Me? No ... hardly at all!' But a little colour crept into her face.

Ruth instantly supposed that the words were regretful. Lester was an attractive man and Jessica Brook might be in sore need of consolation just now. As for herself, there was nothing sentimental in her liking for Lester. 'Why don't you join us for a drink?' she suggested generously. 'I'm sure you need to relax just as much as I do after a day like we've had!'

Jessica was abruptly annoyed with Fate's efforts to throw her into Lester Thorn's way. 'Nice of you—but no, thanks. It's been a long day.' She had no wish to play gooseberry. She did not want Lester Thorn and she would not spoil things for anyone who did ...

She parted with Ruth on the pavement and hurried along to the side street where her small car was parked. She spent ten minutes trying to start it. It had been troublesome for days but this was the first time it had completely failed to respond. She knew almost nothing about cars and had more sense than to poke about inside the bonnet when the Kingfisher must be full of medical students who would come to the aid of a nurse in distress.

She entered the crowded bar, looking for a familiar face . . . and collided with a man who turned from the counter, carrying drinks. It had to be Lester Thorn, she thought with a sense of fatalism. 'Sorry . . .'

Ruth had mentioned the invitation and its refusal. For one insane moment, Lester thought she had changed her mind and he was encouraged. Then he realised the abstracted look in her grey eyes. 'Looking for Clive? I'm afraid you've just missed him . . .'

'No. I'm looking for someone who knows something about cars,' she said, a trifle impatiently.

He smiled down at her suddenly. 'Is there a mechanic in the house, you mean? Well, it makes a change! What's wrong? Is it your car?'

'Yes—and I haven't a clue what's wrong. It just won't start.' She did not mean to be tart. He had a gift for flustering her, she thought crossly. Those very blue eyes and that warm smile could be oddly disturbing when one was determined not to like the man.

'Not in a hurry, are you? I know something about cars. Let me get you a drink and we'll take a look at the patient later.'

'I won't trouble you,' she said stiffly. Ruth was waiting at a corner table, regarding them curiously. Jessica suspected that he was only being chivalrous and she did not particularly want to be under any obligation where he was concerned. 'There's Baxter!' she exclaimed in swift relief. 'He's a car fanatic. I expect he can help.'

'He has the makings of a surgeon but I wouldn't trust him with my car,' Lester said dryly. 'I expect it's only a minor fault . . . it often is, you know. But I'll see that you get home—one way or another.'

'That isn't a problem. I can take a taxi. It's just so bloody annoying . . .' Suddenly, surprisingly, her eyes filled with tears. The seventeen-year-old had not survived surgery. The younger girl had proved to have severe internal injuries and was in intensive care. Jessica ought to be inured to tragedy. But just lately she found herself getting much too emotional over everything.

'You need a drink,' Lester said quietly.

Angry that she had lost her cool and quite illogically feeling that he was somehow to blame, she said crossly: 'No, I don't. I need to get home.'

'Give me two minutes to explain to Ruth and I'll be with you,' he said promptly.

'There's no need for you to be involved in my problems,' she declared ungraciously.

'You don't have to like me to let me do something for you, Jessica,' he told her gently. 'I won't expect a reward for services rendered, you know.'

She was in no mood to appreciate the warmth or the attraction of the smile that accompanied the words. She was unncomfortably aware that turning the other cheek might be good for his soul but didn't do much for her resolve to keep him out of her life . . .

CHAPTER FIVE

'JUST a loose spark plug,' Lester declared, wiping his hands on a piece of old towelling that she produced from the boot of the car. 'No problem. But you really need a new set of plugs, you know.'

The engine was ticking over steadily ... almost purring with satisfaction, Jessica thought dryly, as if it was pleased with the part it had played in pushing her into Lester Thorn's path. 'I'm very grateful,' she said stiffly.

He smiled wryly. 'The timing needs adjusting, too. How long since the car had a service?'

She shrugged. 'I don't know. Too long, I expect. I can't afford such luxuries.'

'Cars are like people. They need a certain amount of attention to keep them happy,' he said lightly. 'I could put a few things right in my spare time. No strings attached. I like tinkering with cars and you'll be doing me the favour.'

'Oh no!' Recalling how she had snubbed him, Jessica was shamed by his generosity.

He looked at her steadily. 'Do you dislike me that much?'

The direct question, so like him, was an embarrassment. Her face flamed and she was glad that the light of the street lamp above them was not strong enough for him to realise her hot cheeks. 'Look, there isn't any point ... I just don't want to get involved ...' She floundered, reluctant to hurt his feelings, not wanting to offer any encouragement to a man she must inevitably disappoint.

He tossed the piece of towelling into the boot and closed the lid. 'Fair enough. I admire a woman who knows her own mind and sticks to it—even if I am the loser,' he said quietly.

She had hurt him, she realised. She did not believe that he could really be in love with her. It was too absurd. But he seemed to be a man who felt things deeply and even if he only imagined himself in love, he could still be hurt by her clumsy inability to let him down lightly. It was not the first time she had been compelled to ward off unwelcome attentions—but she had never been so gauche, so ill at ease, so brutal!

She watched him walk off in the direction of the pub. There was still ten minutes to closing time. Ruth Challis might be waiting in the hope of his return. He would find consolation in her undisguised liking, Jessica told herself, as she put the car in gear and drove off down the narrow street. He did not turn his head as she passed. Jessica felt the meanest thing in creation as she drove home . . .

Her conscience troubled her so much that she found it difficult to go off to sleep although she was tired. It had been good of him to fix her car, risking his valuable hands . . . and kinder still to offer to put it to rights. He had no reason to feel kindly towards her, she thought. He must have a good heart and it was odd that she could not like him.

Would it have cost her so much to be pleasant to him? Would it have hurt to smile, to thank him warmly, even insist on buying him a drink in return for his help? Would it go so much against the grain to meet him off-duty now and again? He wasn't such a bad fellow and there was much to be said for being wanted. At times she wondered if Clive really wanted her at all or if he was merely being kind to someone who was so obviously in love with him!

So Clive had been in the Kingfisher that evening. She had just missed him, apparently. She wondered if he had been drinking with friends or spending yet another evening in the company of Amanda Flynn.

She had not seen him since Suzy's wedding. They had always been on such a casually friendly footing that it could be days or even weeks before he telephoned or turned up at the flat or sought her out on the wards. She was too used to it to think it odd or unusual. She had always accepted his need to be free in the happy conviction that one day she would mean as much to Clive as he meant to her. Loving must bring its own reward in time, she had naively supposed. Now she was ready to admit that her chance of happiness with Clive was too remote to go on hoping.

Clive would be puzzled that she wanted to end their relationship. They had drifted on a leisurely tide of affection and one-sided love for such a long time. Now she was too envious of friends who knew the joy of mutual loving to feel that she could go on putting up with half-measures. But it was not going to be easy to convince Clive that she was in earnest. Perhaps she should encourage Lester Thorn's interest, after all . . .

The thought came just as she was finally drifting into sleep. If she pretended to care for another man then Clive would accept her decision. She rejected the thought abruptly. There were plenty of other men in the world if she needed to go to such lengths and it would be unfair to make use of a man who thought that he loved her. Besides, she did not like him enough . . .

Only the next morning, Clive came bounding up the narrow staircase to her flat. Jessica had just washed her long blonde hair and she went to the door with it wrapped in a thick towel. Knowing his ring on the bell, she braced herself. The moment of truth had arrived sooner than she had anticipated but it was just as well. She did not trust herself not to weaken if she had more time to think . . .

'How's my best girl?' he demanded, putting an arm about her and kissing her on the cheek.

For a moment of weakness, she leaned against him, her heart protesting. Then she countered lightly, as he expected: 'Fine. How are all the others?'

He chuckled, knowing a surge of affection for her. There was no one like Jessica with her warm understanding, her unfailing sweetness, her generous loving. He was a very lucky man. She was lovely, face still flushed from bending over the basin to wash her hair, eyes warm with the welcome that she never failed to offer, no matter what. 'You don't need to worry your pretty head about any of them,' he said, meaning it.

'Oh, I don't!'

Meeting his dancing blue eyes, she knew the familiar tug at her heart. He was such a charmer and so dear to her that it was going to be very hard to part with him. But she knew that she must. They could not drift on with a relationship that demanded too much of her and too little of him and promised nothing for the future. She wanted so much more than he could ever give, she thought sadly.

It was like her not to reproach him or even to hint at hurt feelings, Clive thought gratefully. He knew there was gossip about his affair with Amanda. She was young and impulsive and inclined to be indiscreet— and she was enchanting enough to be forgiven.

Inevitably, Jessica had heard the gossip. If she was hurt, she did not show it. She had never tried to bind him, never protested at his flirtations, never made demands on him. He had always wanted it that way.

Now, unexpectedly, he found himself wondering if it was natural behaviour. A woman in love surely ought to be jealous, demanding, possessive. Didn't Jessica's quiet acceptance, her smiling good humour, imply that she was basically indifferent? Maybe she did not really love him at all.

He shook off a thought that he found oddly disquieting. 'How was Berkshire—and the aunt?'

In six years, he had never expressed a wish to meet her aunt who was all the family that she had ever known. Jessica understood that it would be too much of a commitment in his eyes. She had never minded too much. She did not think that strait-laced Aunt Laura would approve of Clive, anyway.

'Berkshire is always beautiful at this time of the year and my aunt is well,' she said easily. She moved away from him. 'Would you like some coffee?'

'No, thanks. I haven't too much time. Jess, about Saturday . . . Founder's Ball. Will you be heartbroken if I don't take you, after all?'

'Not at all.' She smiled at him. 'Are you on duty?' The chronic shortage of qualified staff could play havoc with the social life of doctors and nurses and it would not be the first time that plans had to be hastily revised or scrapped.

Clive hesitated. 'Shall we say that I'm committed elsewhere?' he said gently.

At least he did not lie to her, she thought thankfully. That would be unbearable. 'I see. You've promised to take Amanda Flynn.' Her tone was very matter of fact.

How well she knew him! And how calmly she accepted him just the way he was, warts and all! There could not be another woman like Jessica in all the world and heaven knew why he found it so impossible to resist the pretty Amandas who came in his way!

'I ought to be hung, drawn and quartered,' he declared.

Jessica could imagine how it had come about. The pretty coaxing of the Irish girl who would count it such a feather in her cap if she could parade a senior registrar as her escort—and Clive's good-natured surrender, his reluctance to disappoint his newest flirt and his careless confidence that *she* would readily forgive as she had always done.

Founder's Ball was the highlight of the year at Hartlake. As many of the staff as possible were given leave to attend if only for an hour or two. For that one night, the hospital ran on a skeleton staff. Jessica had been looking forward to the evening and it had seemed likely that she could rely on Clive to partner her for once. She had felt that she could allow herself that last evening of pleasure with the man she loved before ending their relationship. But it seemed that he had let her down again, she thought wryly.

'We didn't have a definite arrangement,' she said quietly, without reproach. It was true. They had talked about the Ball once or twice, very casually, but he had not asked and she had not agreed that he should be her escort.

'But it's tradition, isn't it? I always take you!'

Jessica smiled at the rueful expression in his eyes. As always, she could not be angry with him. She was much too fond of him. 'Clive, you always mean to take me,' she amended lightly. 'I think we actually went together in my very first year at Hartlake. Ever since, there has been some reason why you couldn't be my escort.'

'Is that a fact?' He was genuinely surprised but he

knew that her memory for such details was much more reliable than his own. He would have sworn that he had taken her to the Ball every year since they had known each other! 'Well, I don't know how you put up with me, Jess,' he said with feeling.

'I don't mean to do so any more,' she said quietly, her heart sinking but her mind quite made up. The break must come sooner or later—and it seemed as good a moment as any. It might be days before she had another opportunity to talk to him in private.

'I don't blame you, darling!' He was light, laughing. He could not imagine a time when he did not play an important part in her life. There was a bond between them that nothing could break—and she knew him too well to suppose that any woman could come between them for long.

'I'm serious, Clive.'

The expression in her grey eyes shocked him into sudden realisation. He looked at her, frowning. 'I think you mean it.'

'I do.' The words were spoken with quiet resolution. For no reason, she recalled the tone of Suzy's voice as she uttered those same words in very different circumstances. Her heart ought to have failed her at that moment. But the thought of the wedding vow that she would obviously never make to Clive only stiffened her certainty that she was doing the right thing. She had given him six years of patient love and loyalty . . . more than long enough for any man to make up his mind about marriage.

His frown deepened. 'Giving me the elbow?'

The words were light. But she knew that he was shaken. It was unexpected—and therefore incredible. She was forcing him to believe her words but he did not believe them. 'Yes, I am.'

'Because I can't take you to a bloody dance? What rubbish!' He laughed without amusement. Dismay rather than anger was behind the vehemence.

'Oh, Clive,' she said with sudden weariness. 'It isn't that . . . not just that! So many things. I can't explain. But we're finished. I don't want to see you again.'

He stared at her, bewildered. 'But why? I don't understand.'

'I know you don't.' She was flat, almost despairing. For he ought to understand. A stranger would be more sensitive to her feelings, she thought wryly.

'Well, I'm trying! It's Amanda, isn't it?' He seized on the obvious but it puzzled him that, of all the girls who had come and gone without affecting their relationship, she should suddenly object to this one. Amanda was pretty and bright and good fun but he was in no danger of losing his heart to her!

Jessica sighed. 'It isn't Amanda—or any girl. It's you—and you'll never be any different.'

He shook his head like a swimmer surfacing from deep water. 'What did I do?'

She smiled. 'Absolutely nothing,' she said, a little sadly.

'Sin of omission rather than commission?' he swiftly perceived. 'I'm beginning to get the picture.' He had been right. All those bloody weddings had made her restless, discontented. He supposed it was very natural for a woman to want marriage. Jessica loved him, after all. He loved her . . . but marriage? He did not think he was ready to undertake so much responsibility for her happiness. 'I thought you were content with the way things have always been,' he said slowly, a little disappointed. He had been so sure of her understanding, her willingness to wait.

70

'There's no point in it any more.' She was very calm. But she was desperately wishing that he would accept and go away and leave her to come to terms with the sudden emptiness in her life.

'You really feel that?' He felt a little sick with dismay. He did not know this Jessica ... cool, unbending, keeping him at a distance with that hard light in the lovely grey eyes. She had always been so loving and giving.

'Yes.' She met his eyes without flinching. Having gone so far, she would not turn back. She had made a stand for the first time in their relationship. His reaction would show, one way or the other, exactly how much she meant to him.

He reached for her hands, held them tightly. He did not make the mistake of putting his arms about her, appealing to her emotions. 'You can't end our loving just like that,' he said, smiling into her eyes. 'We've known each other too long and too well.'

'I don't want to see you any more.'

She said it again, words she had never imagined she could say to him. She must not relent. If she weakened now, it would be nothing gained and nothing changed. Clive did not love her. She was just a habit. She would not be melted by his good looks, his boyish smile, the affection in words and touch.

'My dear girl, you're asking the impossible,' he said impatiently. 'We shall run into each other almost every day as we do now.'

'We can't avoid that. We don't have to meet off-duty.'

His eyes hardened in sudden anger with her obstinacy. It seemed so unreasonable. 'All for a bit of a kid like Amanda! You know how little it means, Jess ... you know me!'

71

'I know how little I mean,' she said carefully and without bitterness.

'Now, that's nonsense! You're my girl and you know it! Darling, you're jealous, upset . . . I've never seen you like this. You've changed,' he said in very real dismay.

'Yes, I've changed, Clive.'

His eyes narrowed abruptly. 'Someone else, Jess?' His tone was harsh with suspicion.

She had been right, she thought wearily. It was the only change of heart that he could understand . . . or accept. 'Perhaps . . .'

'I don't believe it!' He refuted the very suggestion with anger. Jessica was a one-man woman—and he was the man! She shrugged. He stared at her searchingly. Then, reluctantly accepting that it was possible she had fallen out of love with him and into love with someone else, he said slowly: 'Okay. So you've changed. We can be friends, Jess.'

'We've *been* friends,' she said quietly, her tone implying how little that had gained her throughout the years.

'More than friends . . .' His voice softened, reminding her of moments of intimacy.

'Part-time lovers. That isn't the way it ought to be.' Her tone was cool, dry, entirely without rancour.

The colour came up in his good-looking face. 'Look, Jess . . . I'll marry you if that's what you want.' Even as he spoke, he knew his mistake.

'No!' She was fiercely vehement. He did not understand, would never understand!

He was silent. Then he said ruefully: 'No. It was a stupid thing to say . . . I'm sorry.' He meant that the moment rather than the words had been a mistake. He moved towards the door of the flat, paused. 'It's Thorn, isn't it ... Lester Thorn? I knew there was *something*.'

Jessica did not answer. It did not really matter what he thought and one man's name was as good as any other as far as Clive was concerned. It was easier for him to believe that the fault lay with her for ceasing to love than with himself for ceasing to be lovable, she thought shrewdly.

When he had gone, she sat on the edge of the sofa, very still and cold, and wondered why she could not cry. She did not feel anything but the odd and disconcerting conviction that she should have taken this particular step very much sooner. Which was absurd when she loved him so much ...

Later that morning, her blonde hair dried and neatly swept into the usual gleaming coil on the nape of her neck, Jessica drove to the hospital, thankful that she had her work to occupy her mind. Her training and her good sense would enable her to concentrate on nursing and push all thoughts of Clive, the past, and the doubtful future to the back of her mind.

She ran up the wide stone steps of the main entrance to the hospital just as Lester Thorn came down them ... and they both checked in time to avoid collision. Thinking of Clive, she had not noticed him—and he was hurrying to hail a rare taxi that happened to be passing. Late for an appointment, he did not notice Jessica until he almost fell over her. He put a swift hand beneath her elbow to steady her.

'We can't go on meeting like this,' he said lightly, laughing.

Her heart was very heavy. But she found that it was still possible to laugh—and she was rewarded by the swift, warm approval in his very blue eyes.

Remembering that she had been horrid to him, she felt that she had made some amends. 'We do seem fated to bump into each other,' she agreed.

'How's the car this morning?'

'Good as gold!' Jessica hesitated. 'I was really very grateful, you know. I didn't thank you, I'm afraid.'

'My pleasure,' he said quietly.

Her spine tingled. It was the kind of thing that anyone might say. It was not the simple words but the way that he said them, the look in his eyes, the involuntary pressure of his hand on her arm. It really had pleased him to be of help to her and he did not think less of her because she had been so ungracious. It was flattering, she supposed. It was also a little disturbing.

She moved from his touch, not too pointedly. 'Well ... I mustn't be late on the ward,' she said, a little lamely. 'I'm already in Ruth's bad books after last night, I expect.'

Lester glanced at his watch. 'I *am* late—and I suspect that I've just missed the only taxi in town!'

'No car?' she asked curiously.

His smile was wry. 'Would you believe that it wouldn't start this morning? Flat battery. Very foolishly, I left my lights on all night. I must have had my mind on other things.'

Faint colour stole into her face. But why should she assume that he was referring to her? Why shouldn't he have had Ruth Challis on his mind ... or even with him at the time? It was possible.

There was nothing in his words or manner to make her feel that she was in any way to blame for his lack of transport that morning. She did not need to concern herself with his problems and there was plenty of

74

public transport to get him wherever he was going.

'Take my car,' she said on a sudden impulse, taking the car keys from her pocket. 'It's parked about twenty yards down Clifton Street on the right. I won't need it again until ten o'clock tonight.'

He was surprised that she had unbent so suddenly and to such an extent. Very few people were willing to lend their cars to near-strangers and only last night she had made it painfully plain that she had no time for him.

He made no move to take the car keys. She thrust them into his hand. 'Go on! I mean it! You'll be even later if you stand and argue . . .'

At the top of the steps, she turned to watch him stride along the pavement towards the side turning, wondering what had possessed her. She needed to convince him that he was wasting his time in wanting her, she thought wryly. It was madness to give him even the smallest cause to like her more!

It was another busy day on the ward. Jessica had little time to think about Clive . . . none at all to waste on Lester Thorn. She was cheered to find that the fourteen year old Clare had survived the night, after all, and that the prognosis was more hopeful than it had seemed at first.

Late that afternoon, a junior nurse brought her an envelope that 'one of the doctors' had asked her to deliver. She was too junior even to know his name. Jessica glanced at the envelope that obviously contained her car keys. He had scrawled her name on it and, in a corner, the words: 'Parked in same place—how's that for luck?'

Jessica slipped the envelope into her pocket, a little surprised that he had not snatched a few moments to return the keys in person, to thank her for the favour.

It was just on ten o'clock as she left the ward that night. It was raining heavily and she drew her cloak tightly about her shoulders as she hurried along the wet pavements. There were few people about. She felt suddenly depressed as she turned the corner into Clifton Street. It was all very well to be high-minded about dedicating one's life to nursing and putting aside all hopes of marriage—but it was not much fun to be going home to a cold and lonely flat.

As she opened the car door, she was assailed by a heady perfume. Anger erupted from nowhere. She did not mind lending her car in time of need. But it was the outside of enough for Lester Thorn to use it to ferry his girl-friends!

About to throw her cloak on to the back seat, she discovered that it was the scent of roses . . . roses that he had obviously left for her to find. A dozen red roses, long-stemmed and thornless, a very expensive purchase from a very select florist. Shaken, Jessica reached for the card that lay among the exquisite petals.

I love you dearly, he had written.

The tears she had not been able to shed for the parting with Clive suddenly welled and overflowed . . .

CHAPTER SIX

BECAUSE she particularly wanted to see him, to thank him for the flowers, Jessica could not bump into Lester Thorn. He seemed to be the most elusive man in the hospital. She looked for him on the wards, in corridors, in various departments without seeming to look for him at all, knowing the need for discretion. They had run into each other too many times when she had not wished to meet him. Now she could not see him anywhere.

She supposed he must be off-duty. She could not ask those who were most likely to know. She had too much experience of grapevine gossip and it would never do for anyone to suppose that she was chasing him.

Remembering her tears when she found the roses on the back seat of the car, Jessica was just a little self-conscious about meeting him again. He could not know how much they had moved her, of course. It was silly to break down just because in all the years it had apparently never occurred to Clive to surprise her with flowers—or to tell her that he loved her!

She did not want Lester to care for her, of course. She did not believe that he did. He was exaggerating a minor attraction out of all proportion, she decided firmly. She had no desire to become involved with him in any way. But he seemed to be cropping up in her life all too frequently—except when she really wanted to see him!

She returned to the ward after tea to learn that she had missed Professor Wilmot's round—and, presumably, Lester Thorn. She wondered if he had been disappointed by her absence. He was a strange man, she thought, a little irritated. He declared that he loved her and then proceeded to keep out of her way. Any other man would have made an opportunity to see her if only for a moment. He had not even delayed his departure from the ward by ten minutes so that they might meet. He must know that she wished

77

to thank him for the roses that had been so un-expected—and such an unnecessary return for the loan of her car.

So much for being friendly, she thought wryly. Perhaps she had been too friendly, lending him her car. Perhaps he was the type who lost interest as soon as a woman showed signs of thawing.

The telephone rang as she came out of the side-ward where fourteen year old Clare had been taken after surgery and was now on half-hourly observa-tion. Ruth Challis was showing a first-year how to remove sutures and so Jessica answered. 'Paterson Ward . . .'

'I'm glad it's you.'

She knew that odd little tingle down her spine which something in his voice could evoke so strangely. 'Can I help you?' Her tone was brisk. 'Sister is busy just now.' She was aware of Ruth's swift glance, won-dering if the call was merely routine, another emer-gency admission or an anxious relative.

'She's a nice girl. But you're the one that I want,' he said lightly but with meaning.

'You're breaking the rules,' Jessica said sharply. 'You know very well that staff are not allowed to accept personal calls on the wards.'

'I'm assisting in Theatres and I may not get back to the ward this evening. Jessica, may I buy you that drink that you wouldn't have last night? You're off at ten, I believe. I'll be in the Kingfisher, waiting for you.'

'I won't promise to . . .' But he had rung off without waiting for her agreement. Jessica was annoyed. He had phrased it as an invitation but he had not meant to give her the chance to refuse. Well, it would not be the first time that she had stood him up—and for exactly the same reason!

He took too much for granted. He was too casual, too sure of himself. Because she had smiled, spoken, impulsively offered the keys to her car, he thought she was ready to fall into his arms. Well, she would show him that he was mistaken!

'What was it?' Ruth asked, some minutes later.

Jessica paused on her way to the sluice. 'It was for me ... a personal call,' she admitted. 'I'm sorry, Sister. I kept it short and sweet and I did explain that it was against the rules.'

'I don't suppose the sky fell in,' Ruth said lightly, feeling that the girl made too much of a trivial breach of regulations. She looked a little selfconscious, too. She wondered if it had been Lester Thorn on the telephone, recalling that throughout the Professor's round he had seemed inattentive, constantly looking round as though he sought a particular person on the ward.

She liked Lester—and she liked Jessica, too. She suspected that they liked each other more than either of them would admit ...

Just after ten o'clock, Jessica emerged from the hospital and drew her cloak about her shoulders for there was a nip in the air. She resolutely turned in the opposite direction to the pub that was so popular with Hartlake staff and hurried along the pavement towards the narrow street where her car was usually parked.

A piece of paper was tucked under the windscreen wiper. A parking ticket, she wondered, startled. She was parked some distance from the double yellow line that swept round from the main road.

Won't you change your mind?

79

Shaken, she crumpled the piece of paper with his distinctive handwriting and thrust it into her pocket. She opened the door of the car and slid behind the wheel. He was much too perceptive, she thought impatiently—or was she simply far too transparent?

She switched on the ignition, switched off again. Did she want to see him or not? All day she had hoped to meet him for the very good reason that she had been touched by the gift of flowers. Now she was being held back by a foolish independence that resented any man's ability to look into her mind and heart. It annoyed her that he had known she would turn away from the pub and head for her car instead of hurrying to meet him as ordained. It annoyed her that he would look up without surprise when she walked into the pub. Nevertheless, she got out, locked the car once more and retraced her steps along the street towards the Kingfisher and the waiting Lester Thorn . . .

He rose and came forward to meet her with that warm glow in his eyes that fascinated even while it frightened her a little. She was not used to so much intensity of emotion and she wondered if she could cope with this man's passion if she was foolish enough to set it on fire. She must be very careful to keep him firmly at a distance, she decided.

He put an arm about her shoulders and drew her towards the corner table where he had been waiting for her. 'Thank you for coming,' he said, smiling, as she sat down.

She was surprised by that touch of humility. She loosened her cloak. 'I don't know why I did.'

'To give me the opportunity to thank you for the use of your car,' he said promptly.

'You already thanked me . . . with the roses. They

were beautiful,' she said, a little stiffly. She sounded ungracious, she knew. She had meant to speak from the heart. For some reason, everything about him put her on the defensive. 'But you were much too extravagant—and it really wasn't necessary.'

It was almost a rebuke. Lester studied her thoughtfully, knowing he would need to be very patient and wondering if he had only imagined that sudden relenting warmth of the previous day. 'Did you like them?'

'Yes, of course . . . but . . .'

'Then it was necessary.' He smiled at her gently. 'Allow me to give, Jessica. I won't ask anything in return.'

She sighed. 'But you do!' He raised an eyebrow in query. 'Asking me to meet you . . . no, *telling* me to meet you! How could I not turn up in the circumstances? It's a form of blackmail, you know!'

He was silent, considering. Then he nodded. 'So it is. But I didn't mean it to be. I'm sorry.'

She stared, surprised, believing him. He was quite unaccountable! 'I suppose it doesn't matter,' she said briskly. 'I wanted to see you, anyway.'

His heart quickened. 'We progress!' he said lightly.

'To thank you!'

'No need . . .'

'And . . . and to ask you not to do it again!'

He looked at her with a little, mischievous smile in his blue eyes. 'Must I promise?'

Jessica looked away hastily. She supposed any other girl would consider him attractive, would be flattered by his interest and admiration. But she could not help thinking of Clive's laughing eyes and boyish good looks and light-hearted charm . . . and how much she was missing him.

81

She was not at her ease with Lester Thorn, disturbed by his intensity, disliking a certain awareness of the man that tugged persistently at her senses. She recalled that she had toyed with the idea of using his absurd pursuit of her to convince Clive that she was in earnest about ending their relationship. Again she realised how wrong and foolish and perhaps even dangerous it would be to encourage this man's mistaken conviction that she was the only woman in the world for him . . .

'What do you like to drink?' he asked. 'There's so much I have to learn about you, Jessica.'

'There's everything to learn,' she said, sharp because he insisted on turning her name into a caress with that particular note in his voice. 'That's why it's all so ridiculous! The card you wrote last night . . . I wish you wouldn't say such things!'

'Even when I mean every word?'

'How can you mean it?' she demanded impatiently.

'I wish I knew.'

'It's just—fantasy! If you knew me better you wouldn't even like me, I daresay.'

Lester smiled. 'Do you mean to give me the chance to know you better?'

'No,' she said firmly.

'Then we shall never know,' he said lightly. 'And I shall just go on loving you.' He took her hand and carried it to his lips.

Jessica was shaken to the depths of her being. It was odd that a man she scarcely knew should have such an impact on her emotions . . . odd and unwelcome. The touch of his lips on her skin set her tingling. The look in his blue eyes sent a quiver down her spine. The flame leaped, unmistakable, insistent—and she was slightly shocked. She ought not to want him but she did! He stirred her senses in a way that excited and alarmed her and she suddenly knew why she had resisted him since that first encounter. It was not so much that she did not trust him. She did not trust the feelings that he roused in her. Without even liking him, she found him both attractive and exciting—and she was a little afraid of drowning in the dark waters of the passion he could evoke so easily.

In Clive's arms, she had always been more passive than ardent, giving to please him rather than herself. She knew instinctively and intuitively that she could find a delight and ecstacy in Lester Thorn's embrace such as she had never known and might never know with anyone else . . . and it was a temptation to fight with all her might.

For she loved Clive. And there was an ugly name for the feeling that this man awakened in her, she thought wryly. But she had never suspected that sexual need could be so strong, so insistent—or so easily fired at a touch. And it puzzled her that Clive, whom she loved, had never been able to stir her to such fierce wanting.

'What is it?' Lester asked gently, concerned. She was staring at him with something very like dismay in the lovely wide eyes. He wondered what she had seen in his expression to distress her. He loved her. He would not knowingly hurt or offend her. He wanted to cherish her, protect her, surround her with loving tenderness for the rest of her life.

Did it upset her that he loved her so much and could not conceal it? Was she so convinced that she could never care for him? Did she have a tender heart behind that cool, uncompromising exterior? Somehow

83

he was very sure that it was a heart worth winning.

Jessica slowly withdrew her hand from that disturbing clasp. 'Nothing . . .' Her voice shook slightly.

Lester rose, picked up his empty glass. 'I'll get the drinks.'

'Nothing for me,' she said quickly. 'I only wanted a word with you. I don't want anything to drink . . . truly!'

He looked down at her, puzzled. 'Sure?'

'Positive!' She managed a small smile. 'I'm not much of a tippler.'

Lester felt defeated. It seemed that she would not take anything from him if she could help it. He wondered why she had come at all.

Jessica reached for her cloak. 'It's getting late,' she said, rather lamely.

'I'll walk to the car with you.'

'No . . . there's no need.' She stood up.

'There is need,' he said and his tone brooked no argument.

They walked in silence. Jessica's heart was thumping so loudly that she wondered he did not hear it. She was terribly conscious of him although she did not once look at him. He did not touch her and she did not know whether to be glad or sorry. She ached for the touch of his hand. She was terrified of what it could do to her. She wondered if the spark of excitement was the chemistry that everyone talked about and no one could explain. But whatever it was, she had proved that it had nothing to do with loving!

'Founder's Ball on Saturday,' she said, a little too brightly, too obviously making conversation to break the silence. 'Are you going?'

Lester looked down at her . . . and his heart turned

over with the love that had come so swiftly and so strangely into his life. Whatever she did or said, he loved her and he wanted her by his side until the end of time.

'Only if I'm taking you. The evening would be wasted with anyone else.'

As always, he was direct. Jessica found that she was abruptly torn between the longing to dance with his exciting arms about her and the conviction that it would be a mistake to encourage him. Dancing was an innocent pastime but it could lead to dangerous pursuits, she thought wryly. Not really knowing what she wanted, she said nothing.

'Well?' he prompted gently, smiling. 'Am I taking you?'

She was forced into reply. 'I'm not sure of my plans . . .'

'Clive is taking the Flynn girl as she is pleased to inform the world at large. I daresay you know. I think it would be as well if you went with me, Jessica,' he said quietly.

She stiffened with sudden pride. Was he only sorry for her, then? Damn him! 'You mustn't assume that Clive is the only man in my life,' she said sharply. 'I'm not dependent on your charity, you know!'

'*Charity!* My God!' His voice shook. 'Is that what you think? No wonder there's a million miles between us!'

It was the first time she had known him to be angry. He was capable of strong passion as well as that all-embracing tenderness, she suddenly thought, and felt a new respect for him. She had said a silly thing and she regretted it. But she could not bring herself to say so.

They had reached her car, parked beneath a street

85

lamp. Jessica fumbled with the keys and dropped them. Lester bent to retrieve them from the gutter and opened the car door before handing the keys back to her. Their fingers brushed. She shivered. 'Thank you,' she said stiffly.

He nodded, almost curt. Without word or smile, he turned and walked away. Jessica bit her lip. She sensed that he was hurt, dismayed. Why on earth had he fallen in love with her so senselessly? It made her feel responsible to some extent—and she wondered if she had imposed a similar responsibility and that vague feeling of guilt on Clive by caring for him so long and so persistently.

Impulsively, she called after him. 'Lester. . . !'

He turned, came back. By the light of the street lamp, she saw the swift, warm smile. 'I didn't think you knew my name,' he teased gently.

She had avoided it deliberately, feeling that he used her name much too freely for comfort. It brought too much meaning to a very casual acquaintance. She brushed aside his words. 'Do you really want to take me to the Ball?' She could be just as direct and it had its advantages, she decided.

'Yes, of course.'

He spoke warmly without hesitation or any hint of resentment. He was not the kind of man to bear malice, she thought thankfully. She looked up at him with a rueful smile in her grey eyes. 'I don't know why when I never have a kind word for you! However—all right. I should like to go with you.'

'Those are very kind words,' he said, smiling.

'Well, they needn't go to your head,' she warned lightly. 'I'm only using you—and I won't pretend otherwise!' It was true, she told herself, ignoring the fact that he stirred an unsuspected sensuality with the merest touch. She did not want anyone to think that she cared if Clive was flaunting a new flirt—and she particularly wanted Clive to realise that she no longer needed him for her happiness and peace of mind. With Lester Thorn at her side, playing the lover, she felt she could produce a convincing performance.

It was wrong and unfair to use Lester in such a way but she stifled her conscience. He was man enough to realise that he must take his chance of happiness or heartache like everyone else. She had not asked him to fall in love with her. As he had, she might as well turn it to her advantage. And no one could say that he had not been warned!

Lester smiled with understanding. 'I'm glad that you decided to take my advice.'

'Your advice . . . ?'

'To play him at his own game.'

'Oh! Yes, well . . . it isn't that exactly,' she said, disconcerted. She stared at him. 'Don't you *mind*?'

He minded very much. But he did not mean to say so. A man in love must take his opportunities when and where they were offered. He knew she would hurt him again and again. But if that was the price he must pay for a few golden moments then so be it.

'I don't mind anything if I can spend a little time with you,' he said with truth.

Jessica shook her head, baffled. 'I've never known anyone like you,' she said impulsively.

He smiled. 'I've never known anyone like you,' he returned but with a very different meaning behind the words.

She felt uncomfortable. Perhaps she should be flattered but she only felt that she could not live up to the image he had obviously created of a stranger. 'Don't put me on a pedestal,' she said abruptly. 'I'm a very ordinary person with a great many faults.'

He laid the back of his long fingers against her cheek in a brief, tender caress. 'I love you.'

She backed from his touch, tingling. 'Please ... don't!' She was afraid that he meant to kiss her.

Lester laughed softly. 'Try telling the sun not to rise and the birds not to sing, sweetheart.'

It was impossible to doubt that he was sincere. It was rather frightening—and it hurt that he was the wrong man. It should be Clive who looked at her with that particular expression in his eyes and spoke so confidently of a caring that was as natural as living.

'How can you be so light-hearted about it?' she demanded. 'Don't you know that you're wasting your time? You should go away and forget all about me. I shall never care for you, Lester. That's blunt but I don't mean to hurt. I just want you to realise that there isn't any future in it. I love Clive and I'll never love anyone else.'

Lester wondered if she realised the touch of defiance behind the works. Did she truly feel that Clive Mortimer was the kingpin of her existence? Perhaps she did—but Lester needed to prove it to his own satisfaction. He did not feel it was futile to love her, to want her, to dream of marrying her. A man's destiny had to count for something, after all ... and since that fateful evening when they had met in his house, he had been sure that loving Jessica was meant to be— and that he would love her till the end of time.

He brushed a strand of soft hair from her eyes. 'You're very honest. I appreciate the warning.' He looked deep into her grey eyes, searching for the truth. 'Do you want me to go away and try to forget you?'

Jessica hesitated. She ought to say yes and spare him the heartache that was obviously in store for him. She ought not to use him for her own ends. But her emotions were in turmoil. She did love Clive. But her treacherous body foolishly yearned for this man's embrace. It was a very real ache for the kiss and caress of a man she scarcely knew and was still not sure that she liked. It was madness!

Lester's heart suddenly lifted with relief, with thankfulness. She had not said anything but that did not matter. Her hesitation was all the answer that he needed. He caught her hands, gripped them tightly. 'Thank God. . . !'

She was moved. 'It matters that much.' Her tone was very gentle.

He smiled wryly. 'If you care for Clive then you know how much it matters.'

'Yes.' But he was so intense, so much in earnest. Jessica was a little anxious. Loving was one thing but surely this obsession was something very different. How would it end? What would he do when she eventually told him that she could not see him again? That day would certainly dawn. She might decide to like him but she could never love him or want to marry him, she knew. He was just not her type. How would he cope with losing her if she was already so important to him?

Deep in her heart, she had always suspected that Clive might never marry her. He was not really the marrying kind. From early days, she had unconsciously prepared herself for disappointment. She had provided herself with an acceptable alternative to marriage by being a good nurse.

Well, she had warned Lester Thorn and it was up to him to make the most of the little she could give and not look for more. Dependent on his behaviour at Founder's Ball, she might go out with him again . . . or she might not. But, whatever the outcome, she was determined not to surrender to the temptation in his touch, his smile. For that would be an utter betrayal of her love for Clive . . .

She withdrew her hands, said briskly: 'I daresay I shall see you before Saturday.'

'Let me know your address in good time. I'll call for you.'

'Yes . . . yes, I will.'

'Don't change your mind, Jessica.'

Safe behind the wheel of the car, her tumbled senses steadying, she said brightly: 'I won't do that. But you should really be taking a nice girl like Ruth Challis, you know.'

'Goodnight, Bossy-Boots,' he said, his eyes twinkling.

She laughed. 'Oh! You remember that!'

He smiled at her as he closed the car door and stepped back from the edge of the kerb. 'I remember everything about that night, sweetheart,' he said softly, meaningfully.

So did she, Jessica realised with a shock of surprise. And her pulses quickened as she thought of the way he had kissed her—without passion but with a memorable kind of tenderness. Involuntarily she wondered what he would be like as a lover . . . and then hastily rejected the absurd reflection.

She drove off. Glancing in the mirror, she saw him standing at the kerb, watching. As though he was very sure that she would see, he raised a hand in salute before he turned away and strode off with long strides towards the main road.

Jessica smiled reluctantly. She ought to resent so much confidence but it sat very naturally on his shoulders. In a way, it almost seemed like a compliment that he was so sure of her reactions and responses.

But she was not at all sure of the wisdom of seeing too much of a man who was so determined to love her and might too easily undermine her resolution to keep him at a safe distance . . .

CHAPTER SEVEN

JESSICA glanced up from a patient's chart as Clive walked purposefully into the ward. Ruth Challis was off duty and Jessica was in charge.

It was the first time that she had seen Clive since she had told him that their affair, if such it could be called, was finally over. It did not seem that he had any regrets. Everyone was talking about his friendship with a first-year nurse and his unusual lack of discretion made it seem likely that he was seriously in pursuit for the first time in his life. Amanda Flynn had a great deal of prettiness and personality and she seemed to be a universal favourite.

Jessica knew that she should be glad if he could find the right kind of happiness with the younger girl. But it seemed too ironic that he might be thinking of marrying someone he had only known for a few short weeks.

She continued to add the all-important figures to the chart and then returned it to the rail at the bottom of the bed. Pausing for a few moments to talk to the patient, she eventually joined Clive at the desk where he sat, skimming through a thick folder that contained the medical history of his patient.

'Good afternoon, Mr Mortimer. Can I help you at all?' She was formal because they were within sight and hearing of patients as well as her junior nurses. Some of the latter were particularly interested because of the gossip and she wondered wryly if there was anyone at Hartlake who did not believe that she had been more or less engaged to Clive and was now heartbroken by his sudden interest in Amanda Flynn. It was amazing how the rumours could begin and grow and be all over the hospital in no time. Certainly she had said or done nothing to encourage them—and she hoped that going to Founder's Ball with Lester Thorn would discourage the silly speculation. She was annoyed that her private life was being dissected by all and sundry and she could not help wondering if Lester had heard and believed the rumours that were circulating.

It seemed to Clive that her tone was cold and deliberately distant. Was it a reminder that they were no longer even to be friends? He knew that Lester Thorn was easing his way into Jessica's affections. They had been seen together on several occasions and only that morning Clive had learned that she was going with Thorn to Founder's Ball. There was no need to ask her if it was true. Trust the busy and efficient grapevine to know everything about everybody at Hartlake! He did not doubt that Jessica had heard all about his affair with Amanda. It had developed rapidly, partly because he really liked the Irish girl and partly because he somewhat resented the ease with which Jessica had apparently been able to dismiss him from her life.

Six years was a long time and one could not just push aside all the memories, many of them good. They had been friends as well as light-hearted lovers and she had mattered to him. Now it seemed that she had cast aside all that they meant to each other for the sake of a man like Lester Thorn. He had nothing against Thorn, of course. He was a friend. But he would not have supposed him the type to appeal to Jessica who had always seemed to be so much in love with him. How could all that loving just evaporate without warning?

'Good afternoon, Staff.' He could be just as formal if that was the way she wanted it. 'I'd like to examine one of your ladies ... Mrs Lowe? Can you give me five minutes of your valuable time?'

'Yes, of course.' With a slight sinking of her heart, Jessica knew that she was not forgiven. He was a proud man and not the type to take dismissal from any woman with a good grace. He must always be the one to end an affair, she thought dryly—and supposed she ought to be flattered that their friendship had survived for six years and might have continued if she had not chosen to end it. Perhaps he had never loved her although it seemed that she had been more important than most of the women in his life. But she had not been important enough ... and her own pride had suddenly insisted on the break.

She loved and needed him still, she thought unhappily. What had possessed her to forgo the little that he gave when it meant so much? Pride was cold comfort in the middle of the night when she seemed to have little but a bleak and loveless future before her ...

She drew the screening curtains about the patient's bed and stayed while he examined the elderly and obviously anxious woman. He was kind and reassuring but it struck her for the first time that he was just a little impersonal. Perhaps it was inevitable when a doctor dealt with so many patients in the course of his busy day. It was unfair to compare him with Lester Thorn who seemed to commit himself utterly to each and every patient. It was gratifying for the patients and Jessica felt that he was always sincere. It was not just the professional bedside manner that some of his colleagues put on with their white coats. Lester Thorn was really as concerned with the mental well-being of his patients as with their physical condition. But every doctor had his individual approach and Jessica told herself it was disloyal to criticise Clive who was a very capable and valuable member of Sir Lionel's team.

Having finished his examination, Clive went to sit at the desk and write up his notes while Jessica straightened the covers and made the patient comfortable. He glanced up as she joined him. 'The old dear's in pain and we must do something about that,' he said briskly. 'But the Old Man wants some more tests and another set of X-rays before he will operate. There is a slight difference of opinion on diagnosis and I must admit that some of the symptoms are confusing.'

'Mrs Lowe is confused,' Jessica volunteered swiftly. 'I think she mishears some questions and misunderstands others. She's rather hard of hearing and doesn't want to admit it.'

'Well, that would certainly explain one or two of the conflicting statements in her history. But we'll do the tests and the X-rays and prescribe something for the pain in the meantime.' He reached for the necessary forms. A few moments later, he rose. 'Right! Nothing else, is there? I won't take up any more of your valuable time, Staff.' He was brusque, a little angry. Throughout the entire exchange, she had not smiled or behaved as anything other than a well-trained nurse dutifully assisting a doctor. Her expression, her tone of voice, her manner had all been totally discouraging. It was hurtful and it was baffling when they had always been such good friends.

On his way to confer with Sir Lionel about Mrs Lowe's condition, Clive found that he was thinking of Jessica rather than the patient. She was too much on his mind these days when he should be attending to his work or, more pleasurably, dwelling on the undeniable charms of the pretty Amanda.

Knowing that she was currently working on Paterson, he had been prepared for the encounter—but not for its disturbing effect. He and Jessica had been so close for so long and it had been the easiest thing in the world to take her for granted. So it had shaken him to realise that he was missing her very much—and all because of an accidental brushing of hands!

She had passed the patient's chart and their hands had touched. Before, it had always been a deliberate but discreet hint of the personal in the midst of so much impersonality. They had always exchanged a swift and secret smile. But this time it had been unintentional and she had withdrawn her hand so swiftly that it had seemed a deliberate reminder that their long and pleasant intimacy was really at an end. Studying the chart that for a moment did not register at all, Clive had been unexpectedly flooded with regret

95

and a longing to bring her back to her proper place in his life.

But a patient's bedside was hardly conducive to conveying his feelings—and Jessica had kept him firmly at a distance when they did have an opportunity for a private word. He had left her with a feeling of disappointment, of bewilderment. He found it hard to believe that his friendship with Amanda was at the root of Jessica's sudden insistence on breaking with him. At the same time, he did not wish to believe that her equally sudden interest in Lester Thorn could be responsible . . .

Jessica did not doubt that he had much to do and much to think about. But she was a little hurt by his manner, his swift retreat from the ward. With a heavy heart she wondered if her love and loyalty, her readiness to please and her failure to reproach had been more of a burden than a blessing all these years and he was thankful to be free, reluctant to become involved again even in the slightest.

But instantly she knew it was a foolish thought. For Clive had always been free—and he had always been too fond of her to be glad that she had ended their relationship. He was merely respecting her wishes, making things easier for her by keeping his distance, she decided.

Nevertheless, she was saddened. Six years of warm and loving friendship and suddenly they were acting towards each other with all the indifference of strangers. It was not how she had meant it to be—and it was not going to be easy to reshape her life without him. Lester Thorn was a very poor substitute for someone as dear to her as Clive . . .

'Something wrong, Jess?'

Staff Nurse Patricia King, only slightly her junior and a friend from training days, had to speak twice before Jessica became aware of her and reined in her wandering thoughts. 'Sorry, Trish! No ... there's nothing wrong.' She smiled, reassuringly. 'Just day-dreaming!'

'About the new boy-friend? Lester Thorn, isn't it?' Trish sat down at the desk, reached for the telephone and dialled a number. 'I don't know him myself but I've heard that he's a devil for the girls. Watch your step, ducky ... oh, Path Lab? Can I have the latest blood count for Mrs Emily Fowler, Paterson ... yes, I'll hang on. Thanks ...'

Having no wish to discuss Lester with anyone and being much too busy, anyway, Jessica hurried away to begin the routine of the drugs round. It was a slight shock to learn that Trish and probably others had already linked her and Lester as a couple. People were so quick to seize on the slightest hint of a new romance. But there was nothing romantic about the affair ... not where she was concerned, anyway!

Remembering her friend's words as she moved from bed to bed with a cheerful smile and easy flow of light conversation, Jessica suddenly realised a little dislike of a certain implication. Lester was certainly a man of strong and sensual passions although the only kiss he had so far bestowed upon her had been reverent rather than ardent. But a Don Juan, a Casanova? Could it be true? Was she only a possible conquest who was proving harder to get than most? She was dismayed by the thought. Perhaps she should have paid more attention to gossip in the past and then she might have been prepared for that kind of revelation. Trish, like many of her colleagues, enjoyed a good gossip whereas Jessica

97

seldom bothered to listen or contribute.

She supposed it could be true. It tallied with the little she knew of Lester Thorn, after all. He was attractive, very sure of himself, obviously experienced in pursuit. She thought of the seemingly chance encounters, the unexpected gift of flowers, the flattering assurance that he would not enjoy Founder's Ball with anyone else. Any woman would begin to weaken before such a determined assault and Jessica was forced to admit that she had been flattered and moved and even slightly stirred by the intensity of his interest. Now she wondered if all his talk of loving her was just a prelude to seduction . . .

She greeted him with very little warmth when he arrived at the flat that evening. A last-minute rush had kept her on the ward and she was still in her dressing-gown, the filmy lilac chiffon dress that she meant to wear lying in readiness across her bed. She had coaxed her good-tempered hair into a gleaming knot of curls and bound them with a wide lilac ribbon to match her dress. She had just finished making up her face with great care. She was taking pains with her appearance . . . not to impress Lester Thorn but to compete with the pretty Amanda Flynn who would be flaunting her captivation of Clive for all the world to see.

Reluctantly, she admitted him. 'I'm not quite ready, I'm afraid.'

He smiled at her warmly. 'I'm early . . . an impatient lover, you see.' He did not know that his words heightened a faint apprehension that had haunted her mind ever since Trish had uttered those light-hearted words of warning. She was no naive innocent but she had wanted to believe that Lester's feeling for her was not merely rooted in sex. He looked about the small but comfortable room with interest. It was his first visit to her flat. 'Nice . . . do you share?'

'No.' She indicated bottles and glasses on a low table. 'Help yourself to a drink. I just have to slip into a dress and I'll be ready.'

Lester intercepted her as she moved towards the open bedroom door. He sensed that she was ill at ease and it troubled him. Did she distrust him even though he was confident that he had dispelled the initial dislike that had threatened all his hopes. 'Jessica . . .'

No one said her name as he did. It was a caress. No doubt it was all part of his stock-in-trade as a womaniser, she told herself—but her newfound mistrust did not prevent her heart from reacting very oddly to his use of her name. She paused, looked at him enquiringly.

Lester tilted her face with a gentle hand beneath her chin. He smiled into the grey eyes that widened with sudden alarm. 'You're so lovely,' he said quietly.

Then he kissed her.

It was a butterfly kiss, the touch of his lips so feather-light that there was absolutely no good reason for her senses to reel as though a fierce, leaping flame had been fired by the contact. She clung desperately to sanity while her foolish body clamoured to cling to him. She reminded herself hastily that he was a devil with women, not to be trusted, an obviously experienced seducer with his smooth talk and his warm smile and the incredibly blue eyes that would urge her into his arms and into bed if she did not take care!

Lester moved away, loving her, wanting her and knowing how important it was to control the tidal wave of longing that she evoked. He wanted her with the urgency of any man in love. But he was too wise to rush his fences, to alarm her, to take more than she was ready to give. He was experienced enough to know that a touch of tenderness could go a long way towards winning a lover what he wanted. And he was prepared to be very tender, very patient.

Jessica smiled uncertainly, horrified by the tumult of desire that had almost driven her into his arms without a care for the outcome. She was startled. It had been such a brief, fleeting kiss to have so much impact on her emotions, she thought in wonder. It had not even demanded a response! Where was the urgency of passion that she had dreaded and expected to have to repel? It had been the kiss of a friend, a brother, an affectionate uncle . . . and she had anticipated the ardour of a would-be seducer!

She closed the bedroom door out of convention rather than any lingering mistrust. She stepped into the lovely dress and then realised that she would need help with the long back zip. She wriggled and writhed in vain for some minutes before finally admitting defeat. In any other circumstances, she would have called on Liz or one of the girls from the flat below to help. Now it would have to be Lester, like it or not!

She emerged from the bedroom, a little flushed from the futile struggle. 'Could you zip me up?' She was brusque because she feared what his touch might do to her. She was no longer so afraid of him. She was much more afraid of her own reaction to his physical magnetism and wondered how long a woman could be strung to a fever pitch of wanting without betraying it in some way. She had scoffed when people talked of the compelling power of passion that could create havoc in one's life. She would never scoff again.

Lester turned her with gentle hands on her slender

shoulders. 'I've had some experience in these matters, I must admit,' he said lightly, taking refuge in levity because her nearness disturbed his senses.

'So I hear.' The words slipped out of their own volition, tart. She was surprised at herself. Was she jealous of the women he had known, then? It was absurd. Jealousy came of caring, surely ... and all she felt for this man was a fierce physical need that she must fight to suppress. It would never do to yield to such feelings when they were not rooted in loving!

His hands were briefly stilled. Then he said, very dry: 'It seems that I have a reputation that I don't know about.'

'Well-earned, apparently!' The words were meant to be light and teasing. To her horror, they came out like an accusation.

Lester fastened the tiny hook at the neck of her dress. 'I feel as though I ought to be twirling my moustaches,' he said lightly. 'Jessica love, I'm a man like any other. I don't deny that I've taken what's been offered in my time. But that doesn't mean that I'm a villainous seducer of reluctant virgins.' She turned to look at him. He smiled reassuringly. 'Trust me ...'

Jessica felt more at ease once they were on their way. Sitting beside him in the sleekly elegant car, she relaxed and observed him covertly as he drove, capable hands resting lightly on the wheel. They were strong, well-kept hands with long, sensitive fingers ... surgeon's hands. Hands that would always know exactly what to do ... whether wielding a scalpel or caressing a woman into delicious surrender. Hastily she caught up her thoughts. How could she possibly know what he would be like as a lover—and it was ridiculous that she should want so much to find out!

He was very presentable in the midnight-blue suit and powder-blue frilled shirt, open at the neck. She noticed the heavy gold chain that he wore about his throat, the heavy gold bracelet on his wrist. He looked a fashionable man-about-town . . . a far cry from the conservative medical man in the white coat that the patients knew. For the first time, she was seeing him really off-duty and bent on enjoying an evening of pleasure.

He wore his thick dark hair a little long, curling crisply on the nape, waving deeply across his brow. She was impressed despite herself by the looks and physique of a very attractive man. If he was a Casanova then he had everything in his favour, she thought, very conscious of his magnetism and suddenly glad that he was her escort that evening. At least no one could suppose that she had snatched at anything rather than be without a partner, she thought wryly, thinking of some of the specimens of manhood that she knew. Lester Thorn knocked most of them into a cocked hat—and she would certainly be the envy of quite a few of her fellow-nurses!

Aware of her scrutiny, Lester turned his head to smile. He took a hand briefly from the wheel to cover the slender fingers that clasped an evening bag in her lap. 'All right, sweetheart? You aren't cold?'

'No.' She smiled back at him in sudden, warm friendliness. It had taken time but she had decided to like him, after all. She could not continue to dislike someone who cared, showed concern, wanted nothing more than to please and cosset her whatever his motives. And, if she liked him, she need not feel so guilty about the feelings that he evoked.

Physically, she found him attractive. He drew her

like a magnet in a way that she had never experienced before and she was a little shocked by the force of her yearning for him. He was a fever in the blood ... something that she had supposed could only happen within the pages of the most unlikely of romantic novels! Nice girls simply did not yearn to lie in the arms of a man who was little more than a stranger. And she was a nice girl. She had never been promiscuous. Clive had been the only man in her life. Loving him, she had never known regret. But she did not love Lester Thorn.

It was wrong to want him, she knew. It was wrong to feel that if she missed out on the ecstacy that he promised with the merest touch she would feel cheated for the rest of her life. She stifled a tiny sigh ...

The big hall was filled with dancing couples and crowded side-tables when they arrived. Some girls, like Jessica, wore long dresses. Others wore the most casual of outfits. Some nurses were in uniform, just released from the wards or soon to report for duty.

Everyone seemed to be having a good time. Drinks were flowing freely, the music was lively and for once the fraternisation between the sexes and grades was not only allowed but smiled upon. Medical students danced with ward sisters. Junior nurses danced with consultants. Hospital porters flirted with pretty radiographers who would scarcely give them the time of day at any other time.

Jessica sensed a ripple of interest as she took the floor with Lester. She had not supposed that her affairs could be of much importance to anyone but herself so she was surprised that heads turned and people obviously leaned to comment to each other. Perhaps it was Lester's affairs that excited the interest.

For all she knew, they might be legion and she could be just one more in a long line of conquests!

A devil with the girls ... Trish King's words echoed in her ears. *A man like any other, I take what comes my way* ... his own words. She was probably making a very foolish mistake by encouraging him at all, she thought wryly.

Their steps matched perfectly. Lester was a very good dancer with a natural rhythm and a confident lead. Jessica suddenly knew that she was going to enjoy the evening. She loved to dance. Clive was happier to sit and watch, to talk, to drink a little too much. He was not a good dancer and disco dancing was more to his taste because it required little skill. Jessica was pleased to find that Lester could dance so well for she had always enjoyed the pleasure of dancing in close embrace.

He held her close, his cheek against her own, not talking. Jessica gave herself up to the delight of dancing with him as the slight tension of her mood melted away. She had been fearful of his nearness. But instead of the swift wanting that was too insistent, too alarming, she knew only a delicious content in his arms. She floated in a world of soft lights and sweet music and perfect rhythm of movement.

He held her with protective tenderness, steering her clear of the more riotous dancers and those who insisted on doing their own thing to the music, and Jessica sensed that he was cherishing those moments of a new and warmer understanding between them. She was yielding instead of resisting and he was too perceptive not to know it.

It was wrong, it was foolish—but she didn't care! She was intoxicated by the music, the magic, the mood of the moment. Nothing else mattered . . .

The music stopped and people began to filter back to tables and friends and drinks. Lester guided her through the crowd and left her for a few moments to procure drinks for them both.

They looked in vain for an empty table. Jessica leaned against one of the wide pillars that ran around the perimeter of the dance floor and smiled at him over the rim of her glass. 'It's a crush,' she said happily.

He regarded her tenderly. She was flushed, animated, sparkling . . . and no longer on the defensive, he thought thankfully, his heart lifting. She was so beautiful in the floating lilac dress, her bright curls gleaming and her eyes wide with dancing delight. He leaned towards her. 'Everyone is here to admire you and to envy me,' he told her lightly.

She laughed at him. 'Everyone is too intent on themselves to notice either of us!'

And even as she spoke, she looked over his shoulder and into Clive's slightly-frowning eyes . . .

CHAPTER EIGHT

IT was her first sight of him that evening and it was very natural that she should feel a little pang. For he stood by the bar with Amanda Flynn clinging possessively to his arm. The Irish girl looked very full of herself and her cleverness in securing someone as handsome and as important as Clive for her escort. She had also had a little too much to drink already, it seemed. But she was exceedingly pretty with her auburn curls and green eyes and merry little face complemented by the short cream dress that was slightly too sophisticated for her obvious youth.

Jessica was abruptly reminded of the very first time that she had experienced the heady delights of Founder's Ball with the good-looking and attentive houseman of six years before. She had been on cloud number seven just like the youthful Amanda. But she suspected that the first-year nurse was more practical and much less naive than she had been.

She had continued to love Clive long after it became obvious that he would never love her. Amanda would probably know just the right moment to retrieve her heart and look around for a more promising recipient.

It seemed to Lester that there was a stricken expression in those lovely grey eyes. He did not need to turn his head to know what had caught her attention. It was obvious what was hurting her—and he was filled with compassion even while he despaired for his own heartache. He loved her but it seemed that she was determined to go on loving the man who had apparently given her little happiness all these years.

He touched her soft cheek with gentle fingers. 'Jessica . . .'

She looked at him, smiled. Then she moved closer to him, reached to put her arm about his neck and kissed him . . . in full view of everyone, including Clive and Amanda Flynn.

It was entirely out of character for a girl like Jessica. Reserved and reticent, she was a very private person. Her feelings were so mixed that she did not even know what had prompted that impulse to kiss him . . . a sudden warmth of feeling for a man who cared or a sudden rush of indifference for a man who did not!

Yet, as he unexpectedly approached them with Amanda still clinging to his arm, Jessica knew she was far from indifferent—and she wondered what he thought of the kiss that she had bestowed on Lester, knowing how much she disliked a public show of affection. What did he suppose about the friendship with another man that had blossomed so swiftly? Did he assume that she was hiding a heartache with a pretence of interest? Or did he believe that she had fallen in love? Did he care?

He was smiling ... and Jessica knew so well that boyish, slightly rueful smile that touched his blue eyes. He looked directly at her with something very like an appeal in that swift glance. Then he was greeting them both with expansive, seemingly light-hearted ease. He shook hands with Lester, smiled engagingly at Jessica, chivvied them lightly on arriving too late to secure a table. 'Why not join our party?' he continued smoothly. 'It's a little wild but I think you know everyone.'

Lester looked to Jessica for guidance. He wished the man had kept away from them on this particular evening. Clive was a friend but he was very much a rival too—and he cursed the untimeliness of his interruption. For she had been warming to him even if that kiss had only been for the benefit of Hartlake in general and Clive in particular, he thought dryly.

Jessica met his eyes. His expression told her that he wanted her to himself. One part of her wanted that, too. The other part thought wistfully of Clive and the years of loving him and the good times. She knew him so well. He seemed casual, carelessly indifferent. But he was looking to her to redeem a disastrous evening.

Amanda was very pretty but she was something of a

scatterbrain and Clive had never been a man to suffer fools gladly or for long. She suspected that he was regretting his involvement with the girl. She fancied that his patience was a little strained and he could not like the knowledge that most of his colleagues thought he was making a fool of himself over a pretty face.

She smiled and said lightly: 'That sounds like a very good idea. Where is your party?' He indicated the three tables, pushed together, that occupied a premier position close to the dance-floor. She knew most of the group. The seats were all occupied while the orchestra had a brief respite but it was obvious that another couple could be squeezed in. 'The early birds get the best positions. We were rather late.' She allowed her smile to embrace Amanda and walked with her towards the group at the tables. 'Your first Founder's Ball, isn't it? Are you enjoying it?'

Clive and Lester exchanged slightly hostile glances before following the two girls. 'Remind me to do the same for you some time,' Lester said lightly but there was an edge to his tone.

Clive grinned, unabashed. 'Sorry if I've ruined your evening. But did you really think that I'd let you walk off with my girl so easily?'

'You've found yourself a new girl.'

'Oh, nothing serious. You know how it is! A last fling or two before I settle down. Jessica will forgive and forget like the great girl she is,' he said with easy confidence.

'I imagine there's a limit even to Jessica's generosity,' Lester said dryly. 'How many times can anyone forgive and forget that you've led her a dance for years. I think you'll find that you've lost her this time, my friend.'

Clive laughed and punched him lightly on the shoulder in the easy camaraderie of friendship. 'I don't blame you for trying, fella! But she's loved me for years—and she doesn't change. Not Jessica!'

Lester was terribly afraid that it could be true. All the loving and longing that he felt for Jessica did not guarantee that she would not run back to Clive's arms at the merest lift of a finger. His friend's confidence undermined his own. After all, she had been through it all before. Forgiving and forgetting might be as much of a habit as loving, he thought wryly . . .

At the first opportunity, Clive slipped into a seat beside Jessica and spoke to her with an easy warmth that shouted aloud their long and intimate association. She looked at him and smiled. He took her hand and pressed it warmly. The colour came up in her lovely face but she left her hand in his clasp as she turned to talk to the person on her other side.

Conversation and laughter flowed over Clive as he sat, silent and thoughtful, stroking her soft wrist with his thumb in a long-familiar caress.

Watching her as she danced with Lester and then noticing the way she kissed him, he had been prompted by an instinctive jealousy to whisk her away from the other man before heartache led her into something that she would regret.

When she had first told him that their affair was over, he had looked into his heart with care and decided that he did not love her enough to rush into the marriage that she obviously wanted before he was ready. He had told himself that he had no right to protest if she had grown tired of waiting. He must not feel aggrieved if she was looking around for someone who promised more than he did. He had told himself that he must step out of her life as she obviously wanted and leave her free to further her friendship with Lester. For his part, he would be free to pursue the attractive and exciting Amanda with an easy conscience.

But it had been empty pursuit, a salve for the pride that had been wounded by Jessica's decision. Amanda was a sweet girl but she was superficial. She had none of Jessica's warm and delightful generosity, the quiet integrity, the deep and lasting commitment and concern that made Jessica such a perfect wife for any man who was not too blind to recognise her qualities.

Almost too late, he knew why she had insisted on breaking off their relationship. Loving him so long and so loyally, she had despaired at last of ever being sufficiently important to him. She had hoped to shock him into an awareness of loving by breaking with him and taking up with someone else. Well, it had worked—and he was thankful!

He did not blame her for encouraging Lester's obvious admiration and interest. But there was no longer any need for her to do so. He had come to his senses. He knew that he loved her, had always loved her, and that marriage was for him, after all! As for Lester—well, too bad if he had fallen heavily for Jessica. But he could not be too sorry for his friend. He should have known that she was a one-man woman. Everyone else did . . .

Jessica felt she needed a little time to sort her thoughts and emotions into some kind of order. Clive's smile had been rueful, apologetic, and the quick squeeze of his hand had been his way of asking for forgiveness and understanding, she knew. It was so like him, she thought with almost maternal indulgence. Time and again, he had hurt her with a passing infatuation—and then come back to her, knowing she would forgive because she loved him.

She still loved him. So she supposed she would forgive again and they would slip back into the easy, undemanding way of going on . . . until the next time.

Suddenly, pride stiffened. Was that what she really wanted? To be picked up and dropped as the fancy took him for the rest of her life? Clive might never marry her. Perhaps he loved her in his own careless fashion but that was not enough, she abruptly discovered. She wanted much more from a man she loved than that!

He was silent, preoccupied, ignoring the girl he had brought to the Ball. Out of the corner of her eye, Jessica noticed that Lester bent down to speak to Amanda, took her hand as she eagerly rose from her seat and led her out to the dance floor. He was kind, she thought, with a little rush of liking for him. He was sensitive to the feelings of others in a way that Clive could never be. Clive was selfish and single-minded, seeing only what he wanted and pursuing it with very little thought for anyone or anything else. She loved him but she was not blind to his faults, she thought ruefully.

While she talked, she followed the progress of the dancers. Watching Lester and Amanda, she admired the fluid style of his dancing. Observing his smile, his courteous attentiveness to the girl in his arms, she knew that he was a very much nicer person than she had first supposed. Perhaps he was a devil with the girls but she was sure that he had integrity and a good heart. She could trust him as she did not trust Clive, much as she loved him, she suddenly realised.

She wondered if Lester really cared for her as he claimed. It did not seem very likely. She did not believe that a man could love so swiftly and so surely. It was not in his nature. Desire might spark in an instant but a man took a long time to commit himself to loving, she felt. Women were different. Particularly young girls such as she had been when she first came to Hartlake as a student nurse and fell promptly in love with a houseman!

She hoped that Lester did not love her. The more she knew him, the more she liked him. She was a warm-hearted girl and she would not want him to be hurt . . .

Clive tightened his grip on her fingers and she turned to him in obedient response. 'Come and dance, Jess,' he said lightly.

She smiled in surprise. 'Yes—if you like.' He did not usually like. He was trying to please her, she thought warmly. She followed him on to the dance floor and went into his waiting arms.

He was not so tall as Lester, stockier in build, much more handsome to her eyes with his fair hair and boyish good looks and the smile that had always enchanted her. He held her tightly, lips nuzzling at her ear in the way that had always been her undoing in the past. Oddly, she felt no flicker of response.

Over his shoulder, she looked into Lester's very blue eyes, dancing past them with Amanda in his arms. He smiled and winked at her and she smiled back at him with warmth. He said something to Amanda and the girl looked up quickly, responsively, with an eager smile. Jessica wondered if that quicksilver Irish temperament was attractive to him—and if Amanda's pulses quickened at his nearness.

Clive said quietly, tensely: 'I've done it again, haven't I?'

She drew back slightly to look into his face. 'What?'

'Thought I could be happy without you—and soon learned my mistake.' He smiled wryly. 'I've missed you, Jess.'

'You seem to have been much too busy to miss anyone,' she said lightly, coolly. She did not mean to fall on his neck with gratitude as she had done too many times in the past. At last, she was learning. Only that afternoon, he had made her feel like a stranger that he did not particularly wish to know. Now, because he had seen her enjoying another man's company, he had decided to want her again. It was too familiar a pattern!

Reading her mind, he said swiftly: 'Don't blame me for this afternoon! You were the iceberg and I didn't have time to thaw you out. Anyway, I'd just heard that you'd be here with Lester Thorn and I wasn't too pleased about it!'

'You had your plans,' she reminded him smoothly. 'Why shouldn't I accept another man's invitation? We've never tied each other down, Clive. And I did tell you very plainly that we were through. I wasn't surprised that you cold-shouldered me on the ward. It did surprise me that you came across to us this evening.'

'You're too lovely to be wasted on anyone else,' he told her bluntly. 'You must never be anything but my girl, Jess. I know that now.'

'Oh, Clive! You never know what you want for ten minutes together,' she said gently, indulgently.

He touched his lips to her hair. 'I want you.'

Jessica sighed. She believed him. But it was only the

113

mood of the moment. 'Well, I don't know that I want you,' she said, half-meaning it, knowing the way she felt about him would probably overcome the rueful intuition that he would go on hurting and disappointing her until the end of time.

Clive stiffened. Had he pushed her too far this time and lost her forever? Had she found in another man all that was lacking in him?

'Then it is true? What everyone is saying? That you and Lester Thorn are lovers?'

'No, it isn't true!' she said indignantly. But, with the memory of her body's urgent response to the man, she blushed.

Clive's eyes narrowed. 'Knowing him as I do, I'm astonished,' he said, his tone sceptical.

Jessica was abruptly angry. 'Knowing me as you do, you ought not to be!'

Again, that hint of Lester's reputation as a Don Juan, a Casanova. Strangely, it bothered her. She could not expect him to be without experience. But a man who was reputed to be a womaniser might not mean any of the warm and tender and sometimes moving things that he said—and she was suddenly thankful that Lester could not know how her body quickened at his touch.

'I'm sorry. I'm jealous,' Clive admitted. 'I don't like to think of you in another man's arms, Jess. You belong to me.'

Her chin tilted. 'No, I don't,' she said sharply. 'I don't belong to anyone but myself. I'm as free as you are and I like it that way, after all. No strings attached! *Your* motto, Clive!'

He frowned. Then he said quietly: 'Don't let pride spoil what we've always had going for each other—or some cockeyed idea that Lester might want to marry you. He's just stringing you along,'

She smiled. Unconsciously, it was the soft, secret smile of a woman who has been flattered by a proposal of marriage. 'Is he?'

He stiffened. 'He wants to marry you? He's said so?' he demanded suspiciously.

'We hardly know each other, for heaven's sake!' She was deliberately evasive. One confirmatory word to Clive and it would be all over Hartlake that Lester Thorn had proposed and she had accepted, she thought dryly. It was the last thing she wanted!

'Well, you and I have known each other for a very long time—and I love you, Jess!'

'Oh, Clive ...' Her heart was sore. How often she had dreamed of the moment when he might say those words? She had never supposed that he would throw them at her almost angrily in the middle of a crowded dance floor ... and it hurt that the declaration was prompted by anger and jealousy and a churlish refusal to admit that another man could take his place in her life.

She did not doubt him. But she knew that he did not love as a woman needed to be loved. He did not love as a man should love someone who had given him six years of generous love and loyalty, she thought with a hint of resentment. Then, shocked, she asked herself if she only wanted him to love her as a reward for all that she had given. Did she really feel that she was *owed* something that ought to be spontaneous and from the heart to be worth anything at all?

'You don't believe me,' he said heavily.

She laid her cheek against his in a swift, impulsive gesture of affection. Dear Clive. It was not his fault that he was incapable of the kind of love she wanted with all her heart.

'Yes. I love you, too,' she said quietly. But the words, said so often, held very little conviction in that moment.

On the way back to the group as the music ceased, they encountered Lester and Amanda. The girl was bubbling with laughter and excited delight as she clung to Lester's hand and it was obvious that she would be happy to exchange one partner for another at the drop of a hat. Well, he was a very attractive man and he had a way with women that seemed to be irresistible, Jessica thought, almost ruefully.

She was not jealous, of course. Amanda was pretty and personable and really rather sweet but she was very sure that Lester had been attentive to the girl only to sweeten the pill of Clive's obvious neglect.

Briefly, Lester put a hand on her shoulder as he passed behind her chair. Jessica glanced up and smiled, reassured by his touch as she knew he had meant her to be. She felt a sudden affection for him. She covered his hand with her own on an impulse and he bent down to her. 'You're a nice man,' she whispered warmly. 'I like you . . .'

A little smile flickered in his eyes. 'Then remember that I'm the man who's taking you home tonight, sweetheart.' Then he moved on.

Despite the reminder, Jessica might have been tempted to end the evening with Clive if she had been convinced that he really knew what he wanted at last. He was charming, attentive, endeavouring to be possessive without giving a thought to Amanda's feelings—and she was glad that the girl could shrug and respond quite happily to the attentions of other men.

As for herself, she wisely refused to be monopolised by Clive during the evening. She danced with him no more than with anyone else, including Lester, and contrived to convey a seeming impartiality so that neither could take offence.

The last waltz was traditionally for lovers. Clive turned to her expectantly. At the same moment, Lester rose to his feet—and there was an expression in his eyes that did not brook a refusal as he held out his hand to her. Jessica found herself in his arms almost before she knew it . . . and looked back to find that Clive was regarding her in hurt bewilderment.

She refused to feel guilty. Clive had hurt her too many times. It might be good for him to be treated to a taste of his own medicine, she thought firmly . . . and while he obviously had no compunction about deserting Amanda, she had no intention of disappointing the man who had been good enough to escort her to the Ball and every right to expect that she would leave with him. She might even invite him in to the flat for an innocent nightcap, she thought with a defiance that was not at all like the gentle, unquestioning Jessica who had put up with Clive's cavalier behaviour for so long . . .

She toyed with a spoon, stirring the cooling coffee quite unnecessarily, betraying nervousness. Her heart was beating a little too fast. She knew that she was talking too much and too emptily about the evening. She perched on the arm of the sofa, as far from him as possible in that small room, every sense tingling with an awareness of his physical magnetism. He was entirely at ease, relaxed in an armchair. She wondered that she had hesitated at the last moment about issuing the invitation. Had she really half-hoped, half-dreaded that it would lead to amorous advances, she thought dryly.

Lester stood up suddenly. She smiled at him, not knowing whether to be relieved or disappointed that he meant to leave so soon. He took the mug of untouched coffee from her hand and set it on the low table. He held out his hand. 'Come to bed, love.'

She was shocked by his directness. And oddly excited. The look in his eyes spoke of loving and a longing that had become too great to be endured any longer. Scarcely knowing what spell he had cast upon her, Jessica put her hand into that firm and decisive clasp and allowed him to lead her into the bedroom.

He undressed her with gentle and infinitely patient hands for all the passion within him, so urgent that it triggered her own desire. He gazed at her lovely nudity for a long, breathless moment—paying homage. She smiled tremulously, deeply moved by the look in his eyes.

'Lovely Jessica . . .' he said softly. 'I love you so much.' He took the lilac ribbon from her hair and the glorious, golden mass cascaded about her naked shoulders. His fingers trailed gently from the top of her head to her breast via the soft curve of her cheek. She turned impulsively to kiss his fingers as they touched the corner of her mouth. He drew her towards him and gently pressed his lips to her hair, her eyelids, her shapely nose, her cheek, the leaping pulse in her throat, her slender shoulder and the taut curve of her breast.

He was making love to her with the touch of an expert but she ached for his kiss, his urgent mouth on her own. On impulse, she slid her arms about his neck and kissed him. The swift catch of his breath told her that he had been waiting for that voluntary giving of her lips. Then he caught her very close and they kissed like lovers and she knew that she had been impatient for this moment. With a little sigh, she melted against him in complete surrender.

Ardent but tender, demanding but gentle, knowing just how to please and delight, he urged her slowly and sweetly to the edge of ecstacy and finally carried her with him to the exquisite fulfilment.

Euphoric, deliciously drowsy, they stayed in each other's arms, talking softly, kissing, drifting into sleep to wake and make love again ... and Jessica finally woke to the touch of his lips and the bright sunshine of a new day. She opened her eyes with the dismayed realisation that she had spent the entire night in his arms. It had been foolish to become involved with him at all. Now a bond had been created that might be broken but never forgotten. A woman did not forget. If she never saw Lester Thorn again, the memory of him would remain and perhaps a little of the magic would haunt her for ever ...

He had dressed, made tea before he woke her with that kiss. The dress shirt was incongruous in the morning sunlight. She touched her fingers to the faint stubble of chin and cheeks. 'You need to shave.' She was a little shy with this intimate stranger.

He smiled. 'I didn't bring an overnight bag.' He sat on the bed, lifted her hand to his lips. 'I didn't plan to stay, you know. It just happened.'

'I didn't mean it to happen.' Her tone was wry.

'I needed you,' he said quietly.

'I wanted you, too. I'm not sorry.'

Her honesty was touching. He cradled her face in his hands. 'I love you very much.'

Jessica was abruptly troubled. 'I don't love you, Lester,' she said, not meaning to hurt. 'What does that make me?'

He kissed her, hard. 'The woman I want to marry—what else!'

'I don't like myself very much this morning,' she said frankly, a shadow in her grey eyes.

'Do you still like me?'

The tone was light but she knew that her answer was very important to him. 'Yes, of course,' she said warmly, with truth . . .

CHAPTER NINE

SHE did like him, Jessica thought ruefully. She liked him and she enjoyed his company and she was instinctively responsive to the physical excitement of his touch. She had welcomed the lovemaking that had swept her into a new and wonderful world. But it must not happen again. It had been a marvellous, almost mystical experience but it must not be repeated. Sex without love was no part of her code for living, she told herself firmly—and it was something she could never explain away to Clive!

'It's up, nurse—me blood pressure! Gorn right up!' There was a hint of panic in the voice.

Jessica returned her attention to the business of checking the systolic murmur. Mrs Ully was post-operative from a perforated duodenal ulcer and she had been very ill. Now she was looking forward to going home and she was naturally anxious in case any variation in her condition delayed her discharge.

'Nothing to worry about, Mrs Ully,' she said soothingly, knowing the importance of reassurance. 'You're just excited about seeing that handsome husband of yours, I expect.'

In ten minutes, the ward would be thrown open to visitors. Already people were waiting outside the swing doors, armed with flowers and carrier bags and the eager expectation that would carry them over the first and sometimes awkward moments of reunion with wives and mothers and girl-friends who seemed remote beings during their sojourn in hospital.

Almost every woman on the ward, no matter how ill or weak, had made some effort for her visitors, applying lipstick with shaky hands, dragging a comb through hair that suffered from lack of attention, too-long contact with pillows, too many pain-killing drugs. Almost every woman on the ward would make the effort to comfort and cheer the menfolk who were not really managing without them for all the assurances.

'Get away, nurse.' Mrs Ully laughed with a touch of affectionate scorn. ''Andsome? My George? Fancy him, do you? You can 'ave him, love!'

'Thanks very much. But I'm off men for the moment,' Jessica said lightly, filling in the chart before moving on to the next patient. She must finish the round of b.p.'s before the visitors streamed in, the usual job of a junior nurse that she had undertaken because they were short-staffed that Sunday afternoon. She suspected that throughout the hospital there were wards who lacked staff because of Founder's Ball and the subsequent hangovers, alcoholic and emotional! It was an annual problem.

'Stay that way, gel!' Mrs Ully advised with feeling.

Jessica smiled absently. She was almost tempted to follow the cynical advice. It seemed that romance was for the very young, she thought wryly. It certainly did not appear to survive a few years of marriage and the domestic routine and the problems of bringing up the children. That was the depressing part of working on a woman's ward, she suddenly thought. So many of the patients were defeated and discouraged by circumstances, seemingly disappointed with the way their lives had proved to be so different to their youthful dreams. They talked brightly and proudly of husbands and kids but sometimes there was a faint undercurrent of bitterness. Did so many women feel cheated because a tender young lover turned so soon into a very average husband?

Or was love just a myth, after all? Was it only sexual chemistry that brought a man and a woman together and urged them into marriage? If so, then she should certainly forget all about her feeling for Clive and marry Lester Thorn, she thought dryly.

There was obviously more to loving than she had realised. She had lain in Clive's arms without wanting him although she loved him. Last night, she had clung to Lester, wanting him desperately without loving him at all. Perhaps there was another and better kind of loving that she had yet to know . . . an emotion that combined her feeling for Clive with the way she felt about Lester. Or perhaps it was all just an impossible dream. In which case, she might as well give up all thought of marriage to any man and devote herself to the career with a different kind of fulfilment.

As soon as the visitors invaded the ward, Jessica escaped to have her tea-break. Thankfully, she sank into a chair in the senior staff canteen and eased her feet in the sensible, flat-heeled black shoes. They ached from so much dancing. She was tired, too, although she had drifted back into sleep for a couple of hours when Lester left the flat, thankful that she was not due on the ward until one o'clock. But she had been restless, troubled by dreams, and it had been with almost a feeling of relief that she finally threw back the covers.

Idly she stirred her tea with the plastic spoon and memories stirred, too, so that a little colour crept into her cheeks ... and when someone joined her at the round, plastic-topped table, she looked up in the swift expectation of meeting Lester's very blue eyes.

Clive said without preliminary: 'Well, that turned out to be a bloody disaster, didn't it?'

Jessica raised an eyebrow. 'What?'

'Last night. Me lumbered with Amanda and Thorn insisting on his rights.'

She went cold as icy shock trickled down her spine. His rights! Was that how Lester regarded the night he had spent with her—and did everyone at Hartlake know of it!

Unaware of her reaction, Clive went on: 'So it's convention but he might have done the decent thing and taken Amanda off my hands and left me to take you home. He was just being bloody-minded. He fancies you, of course. I don't blame him for that,' he added generously. 'But he's a bit of a lad and I might have worried if I didn't know you so well, Jess.'

She relaxed, her heart slowing down. She was instantly sorry that she had doubted Lester. He was not a man to kiss and tell, to boast about his conquests, she thought thankfully. Not that it was anyone's business, even Clive's, if she had chosen to go to bed with him. But she did not want the whole hospital to know about it. She certainly did not want Clive to know of that swift, almost frightening response to another man ... not only because it would hurt him but also because she would lose him. Clive would not forgive and forget as she had throughout the years. He would never trust her again.

She smiled at him with affection. He seemed bright and cheerful, the eternal optimist, but she suspected a hint of anxiety behind the light words, the easy manner. He appeared to be so sure of himself, of her— but she felt that for the first time he doubted her loyalty. She wondered if the excitement that Lester evoked was obvious to someone who knew her as well as Clive did.

Her smile held reassurance as well as warm affection. He had no need to worry, of course. It was only an infatuation, a momentary madness, a fleeting fever in the blood. Her heart as well as her head was emphatic on that point. It was something that she had never thought could happen to her. She was naturally cool and cautious, level-headed. But it had opened her eyes to a new understanding of the weakness in Clive that had hurt her so often and bewildered her so much.

When he had declared that his flirtations made no difference to his feeling for her, he had obviously been speaking the truth. She knew now from her own experience that a brief affair could be meaningless. She liked Lester, thrilled to his touch, could not regret the exquisite ecstacy she had found in his arms, the magic of that mutual and glorious fulfilment. But he was only a passing fancy. Clive was the man she loved and hoped to marry.

Or was he? Out of the blue, doubt assailed her. Was

it true, she wondered. Or was it just a sentimental habit, a refusal to admit that she could have a change of heart after so many years of loving?

'When can we meet, Jess? Tonight?' He was getting to his feet, leaving his untouched tea, in response to the 'bleep' in his pocket that called him to the nearest telephone.

'I'm working till ten. And I must have an early night. I'm asleep on my feet,' she evaded.

He looked down at her. 'It's important. We must talk,' he urged.

Jessica suddenly knew that he wanted to talk about the future, about marriage . . . and her heart sank. She could not face it just yet. Which was ridiculous when she had waited six years for his proposal! But he had chosen the wrong moment, she thought in sudden panic. Her senses were still swimming from another man's touch and she was no longer so sure of what she wanted!

'Not tonight, Clive . . .'

'When?' The 'bleep' was insistent. 'Jess!'

'I'll let you know,' she promised hastily.

A little shadow darkened his eyes. 'I love you,' he said brusquely, gripping her shoulder. Then he left her, hurrying back to the work that had always been so much more important than any woman but suddenly seemed too demanding when he needed to know how matters stood between Jessica and himself. He had taken it for granted that he was the only man she would ever want . . . but he would need to be blind or a fool not to have seen that she liked Lester Thorn too much for comfort. If she had wished, she could have wriggled out of the conventional commitment and ensured that she did not leave the Ball with the man who had escorted her to it.

Clive trusted her. He knew her too well to suppose that she could be swept off her feet. He did not really think that anything more than a kiss or two had passed between them at the end of the evening. But even that was enough to inflame his jealousy ... and he was determined to stake his claim to Jessica before the world as soon as possible!

Jessica sighed as he strode off. It seemed so ironic. She had despaired of ever hearing those words on his lips. Twice in twenty-four hours, he had thrown them at her in a public place. It did not come easy to Clive to admit that he was emotionally dependent on any woman, she realised. He had been refusing to commit himself wholeheartedly to loving for too long. She could not help wondering if he was really committed at last ... or merely jealous. She had never given him any cause for jealousy in the past. Now her obvious liking for another man might have shocked Clive out of his complacency where she was concerned ... but that did not necessarily mean that he really loved her, really meant to marry her. And she had to be very sure ...

She returned to the ward to help Ruth Challis with the writing up of fluid intake and output charts, filling in of forms, checking stock, answering questions from anxious relatives. When the visitors finally left, it was time for the routine rounds. The evening seemed to drag and she felt a strange emptiness, a feeling of having nothing to look forward to, as she left the ward that night and emerged into the street.

She had not seen or heard anything of Lester since he left her flat that morning. She did not know if he had been on duty that day ... or when she would see him again. Or if she would see him again. She had learned from years of loving Clive that men could be

126

unreliable, thoughtless, inconsiderate. They could walk away from a woman and forget her immediately in the face of other interests. A woman went on remembering long after it would be wise to forget.

Why should she suppose that Lester Thorn was any different to other men? Why should she believe that he cared about her? Men were famous for talking a girl into bed with empty vows of loving, she thought bitterly. Sexual conquest seemed to be an obsession with some men. Lester was a devil with the girls, according to Trish. He was a bit of a lad, according to Clive. Had that been a warning from a man who really did love her and feared that she might be on the verge of falling into bed with a man who was an expert at seduction? Well, the warning had come a trifle too late, she thought wearily.

She slept badly. She woke too many times with a conviction of Lester's presence at her side ... and each disappointment made it difficult for her to go back to sleep. At last, she got up and put on her robe and made some tea. Dawn was just showing above the chimney-pots as she drew back the heavy curtains.

She had the day off. She was grateful for a brief respite from sickness and suffering. Paterson was a depressing ward with so many ill patients. Women fretted, too, about husbands left to cope with all the domestic details and the kids, about kids getting into all sorts of mischief when they came out of school and Dad was still at work, about the length of time it would take before they were strong enough to cope with everything again and whether bored and weary husbands would be patient and thoughtless kids understanding. They were more stoical than men, more resigned to pain and suffering. But they could be more demanding, too.

Men wanted to be up and about for the most part and would do what they could to ease the burden on the nurses as soon as they were mobile. Perhaps because women knew that, once they were up and about, their relieved families would expect them to take over the reins in no time at all, they were more reluctant to take the first steps towards convalescence. And, so little used to being waited on at home, they were apt to take advantage of a nurse being at their beck and call for as long as possible. Jessica could understand and sympathise ... but it did not make the work on a woman's surgical ward any bed of roses.

Her heart went out to the sick women on Paterson but they depressed her. Or was it just the uncertainty of the present and the future that was weighing so heavily on her spirits?

She loved nursing but, in her present mood, she felt like handing in her resignation. Hartlake had seemed like her second home all these years but suddenly it seemed to be synonymous with heartache.

Heartache Hospital, she thought wryly. How true ... and her personal depression was as nothing when she thought of the daily suffering and traumas and tragedies within its walls. How small-minded and selfish to compare the real heartaches of the bereaved and despairing with her own temporary phase of self-pity!

Determined to shake it off, she decided to spring-clean the tiny flat and stock up the larder for those days when she would not eat most of her meals in the nurses' dining-room at the hospital. She did some necessary washing. She wrote to Suzy and wondered if her friend retained any interest in Hartlake activities and gossip now that she was married to Ian and busily settling down to a new way of life. She had promised to pay them a visit but she knew it was much too soon to intrude on their newly-wed privacy. In the summer, perhaps.

She manicured her nails, cleaned her shoes, busied herself with the crossword in a three-day old newspaper ... and finally admitted that she was reluctant to go out because Lester might call or telephone. And that was against all her principles, she told herself firmly. She *was* infatuated if she could think of nothing but if and when they would meet again! She was behaving like a lovesick teenager!

She put on a cream trouser suit to combat the chilliness of the day. The sun was bright but the wind was cold. Without a set destination in mind, she got into her little car and drove away from the narrow streets that surrounded Hartlake, heading for the West End of London.

She could shop for clothes she did not need or go to a matinee of a film she particularly wanted to see or visit the new exhibition at the British Museum or simply stroll through the parks and admire the spring flowers, observing the tourists who were just beginning to flock into the city in their thousands. She decided against the parks. Her feet ached ... and they were always filled with lovers with their arms about each other. She decided against the exhibition—Ancient bronzes were not really to her taste. She decided against the cinema as it was too nice a day and somehow watching a film in the afternoon seemed the pathetic resort of the lonely.

Suddenly she turned the car and headed back towards the hospital. Pauline Ingram was in Sick Bay, recovering from a nasty bout of pleurisy and pneumonia. They were not close friends but they had worked together on many occasions and it would be a kindness to visit, to take her some magazines and cologne, to cheer her up with anecdotes about Founder's Ball and as much of the grapevine gossip as she could remember.

She paused in Main Hall to speak to Jimmy, the Head Porter. The big man with the bubbling sense of humour and a friendly smile was an institution in himself. He had been at Hartlake for thirty years and prided himself on having a flair for diagnosis. He boasted that he could tell what was wrong with a new patient as he or she came through the main doors . . . and he was very often right. He liked to spend his leisure hours in reading medical textbooks and journals so that he could talk knowledgeably with the students and occasionally set them right on a particularly knotty point.

Having been assured that Pauline was still in Sick Bay, Jessica thanked him for information that she had not needed and went on her way, having learned from a glance at the nameboard on the wall behind Jimmy's chair that Lester Thorn was in the hospital and on duty that afternoon.

She did not take the direct route to the Private Wing where a floor was set aside for members of staff who were ill. She went a roundabout way in order to pass the Registrars' sitting-room, her heart thudding with a very foolish hope. It was unlikely to be occupied at this busy time of the day. It was even more unlikely that Lester would have time to relax over a cup of coffee. He was probably in Theatres and she warned herself in readiness for disappointment.

The corridor was empty and her footsteps seemed

130

much too loud. The door was wide open and she glanced into the room, stopping abruptly. 'Hi!' she said brightly, as lightly as she could for the embarrassment and shame that suddenly engulfed her at having sunk to such depths. What was the matter with her that she could not go a single day without wanting to see a man who really mattered so little?

Lester looked up from a copy of the *Lancet*. He tossed the journal to one side and rose. 'Come in!'

Jessica hesitated in the doorway. 'What! Enter the holy of holies? That will start tongues wagging,' she said, smiling. Her heart was pounding in her throat. He was really much too attractive, she thought ruefully.

'I'm alone. Close the door and no one will know that you're here with me.'

'Strictly forbidden, doctor!' she exclaimed in her best imitation of Sister Booth.

Lester smiled. 'Rules were made to be broken.'

'Not by me! I'm an exemplary nurse!'

'Let me tempt you,' he said softly. She raised an amused eyebrow. His smile deepened. 'The coffee is fresh.'

Jessica promptly closed the door and perched on the arm of a chair. 'I'm tempted!' He poured coffee and brought the cup to her. She took it, wondering if he knew that her heart was beating too fast for comfort or common-sense. 'How are you?' She looked up at him with a smile, wondering if she only imagined a slight coolness in his manner. Was it her consciousness—or was he really just a trifle distant for all the seeming friendliness? They were still strangers, she thought wryly. They knew very little about each other although she had lain in his arms and thrilled to his kisses, his expert lovemaking.

'I'm fine.' He returned to his former chair. 'I like the new uniform. It suits you.'

'Idiot!' she teased, not really at ease but trying to be. 'Don't you know that this is what the well-dressed nurse about town wears when she's off duty?'

'I knew you were off duty,' he agreed.

Jessica glanced away from those blue eyes, slightly disconcerted. Was she being too obvious? Or was he merely too perceptive? She suddenly felt sure that he had deliberately not been in touch . . . either because he was not free to meet her or because he had abruptly lost interest. It was horrible not knowing what to believe.

'So what are you doing here?' he asked, his eyes crinkling with amusement. 'Apart from drinking the coffee that is traditionally sacred to hard-working Registrars.'

'Visiting the sick. Pauline Ingram. Do you know her? She's in Sick Bay and I thought I'd spend a little time with her this afternoon.'

'You do love your work, nurse,' he teased gently.

Jessica felt that he knew exactly what had brought her to the hospital on her day off. Colour rushed into her face. 'Oh, I'm very dedicated,' she returned lightly. 'I mean to be Matron one day.'

'Marriage will get in the way of that admirable ambition, I imagine.'

'Oh, I don't know. Being married doesn't appeal very much,' she said airily.

'To Clive? Or to me . . .?'

The direct question took her by surprise. She did not know how to answer. She did not know if it was a serious proposal or a joke. For one incredible moment, she was not even sure which she wanted it to be!

She took refuge in levity. 'If I ever decide to get married I won't take anyone less than a consultant!'

Lester felt that she had answered him in a round-about way. For everyone knew that Clive Mortimer was working towards a consultancy and no one doubted his eventual success.

Only that morning, Clive had informed a roomful of colleagues that he was soon to be married ... and Lester had known that there was a warning intended for him behind the words. Clive had backed away from premature congratulations. No date was fixed, he hadn't even bought the ring yet, certainly it was Jessica Brook—who else? Of course she would marry him! She'd been waiting for years for him to pop the question. Amanda Flynn? A last *flynn*, he had declared ... and the execrable pun had been greeted with groans.

Lester had left the room, unobserved. He did not doubt that Clive had finally made up his mind to marry Jessica. But was she still set on marrying him, he had wondered. Now her flippant response to his question seemed to confirm the dismaying suspicion that she would never belong to him.

'Then I won't do for you,' he said smoothly. 'I'm going to be a back-room boy. I've been offered a job in the new Research Unit at the Central.' The offer existed. It was a sudden decision to accept.

'You're leaving Hartlake?' Dismay sprang to eyes and voice.

Lester smiled with sudden warmth, his spirits lifting. He was not so foolish as to suppose that one night in his arms could erase the years of loving she had bestowed on another man. Warm and generous, much too impulsive, she had obviously yielded to the excitement and enchantment of the moment. But, like any lover, it was impossible for him not to hope for some

kind of miracle and he was heartened by that involuntary reaction.

'Not just yet . . . and the Central isn't on the other
side of the world, Jessica love,' he said gently.

Her heart quivered at the endearment she had come
close to wondering if she would ever hear again. 'No.
Of course not . . .' She put the untouched coffee on a
low table.

Lester reached for her hand, drew her down to his
knee. She resisted for only a moment. They kissed and
she wondered if he knew how her heart thudded, how
the blood quickened in her veins, how her body leaped
with wanting. So much for all her resolution, she
thought ruefully. He had only to touch her and she
was engulfed with longing. His kiss, his hand on her
breast, the urgency that matched her own, was a quite
irresistible enchantment . . .

The door opened abruptly. For a moment, the
stocky, fair-haired surgeon in the green operating
gown stood in the doorway, studying them . . . and
then he went quietly away.

CHAPTER TEN

Jessica leaped to her feet in dismay. 'That was Clive!'
she exclaimed.

'Then we are luckier than we deserve to be,' Lester
told her, smiling. 'It could have been Matron—or my
boss!'

'You don't understand!' She was sharp, annoyed by
his lack of concern. But of course it would not matter
to him if Clive never spoke to her again!

134

Lester surveyed her thoughtfully. Her dismay told its own story, he decided wryly. 'I understand only too well,' he said quietly. He ran a hand through his dishevelled dark hair.

Unconsciously, Jessica raised a hand to her own head. But the smooth chignon had not been disturbed by those brief moments, so magical, so rudely interrupted, so much regretted. For she was much too fond of Clive to want him hurt or humiliated despite his own weakness and careless disregard of her feelings in the past.

'I wish it had been anyone but Clive!' Her tone was rueful.

Lester raised an eyebrow. 'Even Matron?' he teased gently.

She was in no mood to make light of the matter. 'Even Matron! I can survive her displeasure. I'm a qualified nurse. I can always find another job,' she declared impatiently.

He was silent, digesting the words, disliking the implications of that dismay and concern. It seemed that nothing was as important to her as Clive . . . and certainly not himself. At last he said quietly, a little wryly: 'But not another Clive. That's really what you're saying, isn't it?'

Jessica hesitated. He was too direct, forcing her into a corner, urging her to commit herself . . . and she was far from sure what she really wanted. Lester was very nice, very attractive and exciting. She liked him a lot. But Clive had been an important part of her life too long for her to readily visualise a future without him. It was really a very difficult decision and she resented having to choose between them. It seemed absurd that she could not have them both as friends, she thought with a very natural impatience. But they both wished to be lover rather than friend and each looked upon the other as a rival. It made life much too complicated and she was almost tempted to be done with both of them and devote herself entirely to nursing!

'I don't expect you to like the way things are,' she said slowly, wishing that he did not love her and must inevitably be hurt by the preference for Clive that she could not help.

'Letting me down lightly, love?' he asked swiftly, a wry smile quirking his lips. His tone was light but his heart was heavy with the pain of loving a girl who did not seem to know what she wanted. It had not seemed to him during those memorable hours when she had lain in his arms or just now when she had responded so eagerly to his kiss that she could be so much in love with another man. He had not made the mistake of supposing that she was near to loving him, either. But he had allowed himself to hope.

'He means a lot to me,' she said, a little desperately for she was troubled with guilt at the thought of how much she had encouraged the wrong man to love her and how much she needed his understanding of her inner conflict.

'And I don't.' The words were blunt but without reproach.

Jessica met the very blue eyes with their compelling reminder of magic moments. If only she had not yielded to the intoxicating excitement in his touch, she thought ... even as she knew in the depths of her being that it was impossible for her to regret having known him. One went through life storing up lovely memories against a doubtful future and if she never saw him again she must always remember this man with tenderness.

She sighed. 'I'm not sure how I feel about you,' she admitted ruefully.

'That's honest, anyway.' He smiled at her with sudden warmth.

Her heart gave a little lurch. But she reminded herself firmly that he was still the unknown quantity. Clive, for all his faults, was very familiar and very dear.

She said steadily, anxious to be fair: 'Clive and I have known each other such a long time, Lester. We've been very close all these years.' His eyes looked intently into her own and a little colour stole into her face. 'It doesn't mean that you and I can't be friends, surely?'

'Cold comfort,' he said quietly. 'I love you.' It was not a plea but a quiet statement of fact.

'So does Clive,' she said carefully, not trying to hurt but feeling that he ought to be warned against hoping. For while her emotions might be so topsy-turvy now it was very possible that her natural caution would win the day. For what did she really know of Lester Thorn? And she had known Clive so long and so well . . .

'Then may the best man win.' Lester strove for lightness, knowing that a woman could be persuaded into loving but never forced. He smiled at her with infinite tenderness. 'Don't look so troubled, Jessica love. You have only to make up your mind which of us you want, you know. Is that so difficult?' His tone was gentle.

It was much more difficult than he could know, she thought wryly. For he endeared himself to her in so many ways. But her feeling for Clive had surely stood the test of time and she could not help feeling that it could be merely physical attraction that drew her so strongly towards this man.

Again she felt as if he was pushing her into a decision before she was ready. She said impulsively, a little impatiently: 'Oh, I do wish that Clive hadn't walked in at just that moment!' She did not realise that her tone reproached Clive for unwittingly bringing matters to a head.

'Does it really matter so much? He knew of our friendship from the beginning.'

'Yes—but he thought it was only friendship,' she pointed out swiftly. 'Now . . . oh, he must be shattered!'

'The image is shattered, certainly,' Lester agreed dryly. 'Not a bad thing, perhaps. But you can't blame him for taking you for granted—and you can't expect him to like it when you deviate from the norm. After all, he staked his claim to you years ago, didn't he— and you've been dangling on a string ever since, just waiting for him to notice you whenever he's at a loose end. You've convinced him and everyone else that he only has to say the word and you'll marry him.'

Her chin tilted in swift dislike of that faintly critical representation of her loving patience and loyalty. She wondered if everyone at Hartlake thought her weak and foolish, clinging to an empty dream. Lester obviously did. 'That's probably true,' she said on a little spurt of pride.

Lester looked at her with a thoughtful expression in his eyes. 'Yes, it probably is,' he said heavily. 'You're so bloody stubborn, sweetheart.'

'I happen to love him,' she declared tartly, defensively—and refused to question if it was true. Of course she loved Clive. Always had, always would!

She was not the kind of girl to fall out of love just because one man did not quite measure up to a romantic ideal and another man was too attractive for anyone's good!

Lester walked to the window that overlooked the hospital garden and Sir Henry's statue. His hands clenched in the deep pockets of his white coat and a nerve jumped in his lean cheek. He could feel her slipping away from him—and all for the sake of a misguided sense of loyalty and a ridiculous pride that could not admit to mistake.

A first-year nurse hurried through the garden with an armful of folders and a harassed expression. She was very young.

'Come here.' Startled into obedience by something in his voice, Jessica went to stand by him. He put a light arm about her shoulders. 'You know as much about loving as that junior knows about open-heart surgery,' he said quietly. 'She might learn with time. But I'm beginning to despair of you, love.'

She sighed. 'I wish you would accept . . .'

He smiled wryly. 'Frustrating, isn't it? I know the feeling.'

'I did warn you,' she reminded him.

'Yes, you did. But it was much too late, you know.' He touched his lips to her soft hair and then released her. 'I expect you want to find Clive,' he said lightly.

'I wish I knew what to say to him,' she said, wryly.

Lester looked down at her with a hint of tenderness in his blue eyes. 'Blame everything on me. Say that you were looking for him and I took advantage of you in an unguarded moment. He'll believe it.'

Jessica looked doubtful.

Clive probably would believe it, she thought . . .

because Lester was reputed to be 'a bit of a lad' and because she was generally described as an iceberg. She could scarcely believe herself that she had gone so readily into those arms when both time and place were so unsuitable. It had been inevitable that someone should walk in on them. It was particularly unfortunate that it should have been Clive.

He would believe anything she cared to tell him. But she hesitated to opt out of all responsibility for something that she had both invited and enjoyed.

'But it wasn't like that,' she demurred.

Lester smiled. If only she was as honest when she looked into her heart, he thought ruefully. She had been believing herself in love for so long that she just didn't know how to stop. Perhaps she had loved Clive at one time—when she was too young to know the difference between calf love and the real thing. Lester was convinced that it was no more than sentimental habit, six years later.

He thought of her warmth and sweetness, her wholly generous response to his lovemaking, and he was convinced that she would not have allowed him into her arms and into her bed if she was in love with another man. She was simply not that kind of woman. Whether she knew it or not, Clive belonged to the past. Lester hoped with all his heart that she would eventually realise that he was the man for her future.

He smiled, eyes crinkling in the way that had caused many a susceptible heart to quicken. 'It's your choice,' he said lightly. 'You can tell the truth. Or you can lie a little and make the man happy.'

'Yes . . .' Jessica picked up her bag, slung it over her shoulder and moved slowly towards the door.

She needed to see Clive, to talk to him, to put things

right between them, of course. At the same time, she realised that it could be the parting of the ways for herself and Lester. For all the lightness of his tone, it was an ultimatum. *Make Clive happy if you must,* he was saying—*but don't expect anything more from me.* And he had sufficient strength of mind and character to turn away even though he loved her, she realised with an odd little pang. He would admit defeat if she ran back to the doubtful security of Clive's arms. He would not swallow his pride, endure any amount of humiliation, cling to false hopes just because he loved. He would walk out of her life and learn to live without her—and one day he would love again.

Jessica was dismayed to realise that she was being tugged in two directions. She loved Clive. But she would really miss Lester . . .

She told herself firmly that she would only miss the quivering excitement, the sensual delight, that had little to do with real loving. She had been quite content until she knew him and she could be so again. Clive might be weak and a little selfish and sometimes thoughtless but for six years she had centred all her hopes and dreams on him. It would be madness to allow a foolish infatuation to ruin a future that had been planned long before she became aware of Lester Thorn's existence!

She paused by the door, looked at him with regret in her grey eyes. She had not wanted to hurt him. But it was not her fault that he had loved her without the least encouragement. 'I'm sorry . . .'

His eyes darkened with pain. He had lost her, he knew. Whatever her reasons, she was determined to cling to an absurd ideal of love that she had cherished much too long. 'So am I,' he said gently. 'For us both . . .'

Jessica hurried along the corridor, fighting the ridiculous impulse to go back and hurl herself into his waiting arms. She told herself sternly that she ought to know what she wanted after six years. She was twenty-four, a grown woman, matured by years of nursing and much too level-headed to allow her life to be ruined by an ephemeral emotion.

Perhaps she had been too dedicated to her work, too intent on being a good nurse, too determined to keep every man but Clive at a safe distance. Perhaps she should have flirted a little, slept around like other girls—and then she might have known how to cope with the feelings that Lester evoked, just how little importance to attach to them.

As it was, she had been swept off her feet by an emotional experience such as she had never known with Clive—and come dangerously near to fancying herself in love! Which was absurd when the way she felt about Lester was nothing like the love for Clive that she had cherished for years. She could only be thankful that she had recognised mere physical attraction for what it was and not sacrified her real happiness for it, she told herself.

It took some time before she traced Clive to Accident and Emergency where he had been called for a consultation. He was engaged in an earnest discussion with a junior doctor. As Jessica pushed through the swing doors into the busy department, he glanced up from his scrutiny of the patient's notes and their eyes met. She smiled tentatively. Clive nodded briefly, a mere acknowledgment that gave nothing away, and went on outlining a course of action to the houseman who listened with eager and deferential attention.

Out of uniform, Jessica felt oddly unsure of herself. Waiting for Clive's attention, she wondered if the patient people on the long benches assumed her to be one of their own kind or an anxious relative. She suddenly realised how much she depended on her cap and apron for confidence and self-assurance.

Wearing the famous Hartlake uniform she was cool and competent, briskly efficient, knowing exactly what to do and how to do it, in command of every situation. Out of uniform, she was a poor thing, she thought wryly . . . going to pieces at the first threat of disruption to the orderly running of her life.

She sat down on a bench to wait until Clive was free to talk. A fair-headed little boy approached her with the easy friendliness of the infant and she smiled at him, leaned down to speak to him, admired the toy car he had brought to show to her. There was something about him that made her think of Clive . . . the sturdy frame, the mop of fair hair, the cheerful smile and the confidence of his approach. He stirred her maternal instincts and she wondered if she would ever carry Clive's child. Marriage meant motherhood . . . but it was difficult to imagine Clive in the role of father. In some ways, he was still a child himself, she thought with affectionate indulgence.

She realised that the easy, undemanding friendship with Clive had been a comfortable background to her nursing career. She was not a frivolous or flirtatious girl and so did not appeal to most of the young doctors at Hartlake who liked the company of a pretty and personable nurse but had no wish to become emotionally involved. Clive was the kind of man who could be loved without feeling obliged to reciprocate or break off the relationship—and Jessica had allowed him to suppose that she was content with the occasional scrap of his attention.

She had been content, she amended fairly. She had not been anxious for an early marriage with the demands and responsibilities that might have taken her away from the nursing that she loved. Loving Clive at the same time had made few demands on her emotions and energies, never interfered with her work on the wards and had absolved her from the almost compulsory flirtations indulged in by most of her set. It had been a convenient arrangement in many ways.

So perhaps it was not surprising that Lester's passionate intensity had been disturbing, alarming. It had seemed a threat to the even tenor of her routine-filled life. He was no easy-going, undemanding lover like Clive, giving little and asking little. He gave all that he had—and demanded more from her than she was perhaps capable of giving, she decided.

In her heart, she knew that she had run away from the challenge of his love. She felt safer with Clive. She knew just where she was with Clive. She need not be afraid of hurting and disappointing Clive whose kind of loving was so familiar and comfortable.

The young mother swooped on her little boy and scolded him for pestering and then swept him into a cubicle as a nurse beckoned . . . and Jessica scarcely had time to bestow a reassuring smile on her new friend.

Clive moved away from his colleague who went into the cubicle where his patient was waiting for reassurance . . . and Jessica rose to intercept him before he could push his way through the swing doors as she half-expected. Instead he came towards her, smiling.

'Hallo, darling.' His greeting was light and warm as

though he had never seen her in that intimate embrace.

'Clive, can we talk?' she said anxiously. 'I know you must be busy but . . .'

'I'm rushed off my feet,' he agreed. 'But I can always find time for you.' He put an arm about her waist, careless of curious glances, of nudging elbows, of amused speculation among the waiting patients and attendant staff.

Jessica was a little puzzled. Was he determined to pretend that he had not seen her with Lester—or was he totally unaffected by it all? She was relieved by his easy manner, his apparent lightness of heart. At the same time, it was disconcerting. Did he attach so little importance to her liking for another man? Was he so sure of her? Woman-like, she was vaguely irritated by such male arrogance.

She moved from his encircling arm. She had never liked public display of affection and it seemed particularly out of place in Accident and Emergency with its serious and often tragic overtones.

A first-year nurse came towards them, pushing a cheerful young man in a wheelchair, en route for the X-ray Department. He had broken both ankles after falling from the roof of a house on a building site. The girl knew Jessica and she smiled in passing and glanced curiously at Clive, still in surgical gown and boots where he had been called down from Theatres.

Curtains were whisked back from one of the cubicles and a porter wheeled an old lady on a trolley towards the lifts, talking cheerfully to the patient despite the tears that streamed down her lined face. A nurse accompanied them, carrying the big plastic bag that contained the patient's clothes, and armed with a folder that listed as much detail as they had managed to elicit from the confused victim of a road accident. She had walked into the path of a car but was more shaken than hurt. She was being admitted for observation.

A distraught young mother came in with a screaming toddler clinging to her skirt and a too-still baby clutched to her breast. They were escorted by a kindly ambulanceman and they were obviously expected. He had radioed en route to the hospital. A nurse came hurrying to take the baby from its mother and whisk it into a cubicle and a dark-skinned woman doctor followed to give emergency treatment with unhurried efficiency.

'Not here . . .' Jessica said quickly, feeling that her own affairs were trivial in comparison with the dramas that were daily enacted within the hospital walls.

Clive's mouth tightened fractionally as she jerked from his touch. She had not been so reluctant in Thorn's embrace, he thought savagely. Did she think it was easy for him to smile, to talk to her, to put an affectionate arm about her as though he was unaffected by her feeling for another man?

He glanced at the big clock. 'I'm due to assist the Old Man with a valve replacement in twenty minutes,' he said lightly. 'I ought to get back to Theatres and scrub-up. Walk with me, Jess. We can talk on the way.'

She preceded him through the swing doors, wondering if there was sufficient time to apologise, to explain—and wondering if there was any need when he seemed so unconcerned about the whole thing.

In fact, Clive was very concerned. Loving her, needing her, he was determined not to let her go. For the moment, she might believe herself in love with Lester but it could only be a passing fancy. Jessica was the faithful kind, a one-man woman. Seeing them together, he had realised that she was more involved than he had known. But he suspected that it was only an unconscious rebellion after six years of loving him with so little to show for it. It had been triggered by Suzy's wedding and his own clumsiness, he thought wryly. Looking back, he knew and regretted the many humiliations he had heaped on her throughout the years. Well, he was ready to spend the rest of his life in making it up to her . . .

Jessica turned to him with a rueful expression in her grey eyes. 'What must you think of me?' she said without preliminary. For they were friends and where was the need to beat about the bush?

Clive was annoyed. Why couldn't she play it his way, he thought irritably. Trust Jessica with her sometimes inconvenient honesty to drag everything into the open! Least said soonest mended had always been his motto.

'I think you take things too seriously, Jess,' he said smoothly, smiling at her indulgently.

She was baffled by his coolness. She stared at him. 'I thought you were upset, angry,' she said slowly.

'Well, I'm not delighted,' he admitted bluntly. 'But these things happen—and they're best forgotten. Unless you're trying to tell me that you love the fellow!'

She shook her head. 'No.'

'Then it doesn't mean much, does it? No more than my little whirl with Amanda.' He wished he could believe it. Involvement with other girls had always been easy for him, light loving that meant little, a kind of relaxation that was important to a man who spent long and arduous hours on the serious business of surgery. But Jessica had never indulged in casual affairs. He paused, looked down at her with serious eyes. 'I think it's time I put a ring on that finger, Jess,' he said, taking her left hand and separating the slender ring finger from the others. 'A diamond for starters. It will keep the Casanovas away and remind me not to be such a bloody fool in future.'

Jessica's heart almost stopped. But not with delight. For the words, so unexpected and so long-awaited, only filled her with dismay.

'I believe you're proposing!' she exclaimed, trying to smile, trying to turn it into a joke. For she was not ready to marry him, she thought in sudden panic. She did not want to marry anyone just yet . . . least of all the man that she had loved for so long.

'I should have done it years ago,' Clive said warmly, meaning it.

She thought wryly that only a few weeks before she would have been dancing on air. Now she was unsure, hesitant, afraid to trust him with something as precious as her happiness.

'But, Clive . . .'

He silenced her with gentle fingers on her lips. 'It's what you've always wanted, isn't it, Jess?'

She could not deny it. 'Yes, of course.' She made another effort. 'But, Clive.'

'Love me?' he asked softly, confidently.

The boyish smile had always caught at her heart, weakened her resistance, stilled all her doubts. He was a charmer and she had loved him so long.

Jessica stifled the small voice of protest in her heart. She nodded, smiled at him, said weakly: 'You know I do.'

148

But the words that she knew he wanted to hear were held back by an innate honesty that forced her to recognise that there was loving and *loving* ... and she was no longer so sure which of them she felt for the man who expected her to marry him.

CHAPTER ELEVEN

THE news spread like a forest fire.

When she arrived on duty the following day, Jessica was surprised to discover how many people knew of her engagement to Clive—and how many of them wished her well. She had not realised that she was well-liked by her colleagues and she had supposed that they took only an indifferent interest in her affairs. Now she learned that her hope of marrying Clive had been common knowledge and everyone was delighted for her that a dream had finally come true.

It was difficult for her to be so delighted. But she realised that it could only be reaction. Very often, the realisation of a dream could be something of an anti-climax. It could even seem like a let-down, temporarily. She would soon begin to feel all the normal emotions of a newly-engaged girl. In the meantime, she must not let Clive suspect how little it meant to her to be planning their wedding.

He wished it to be very soon, surprising her with his impatience. Now that he had finally made up his mind to sacrifice his freedom on the altar of marriage, it could not apparently be soon enough for him. Jessica, consciously playing for time, pointed out that her aunt would certainly want to give her a white wedding with all the trimmings and such things took time to organise. Also they would have to find somewhere to live that was convenient for Hartlake as she wanted to carry on nursing for the time being. Her flat was much too small and he shared the top half of an old house with two other doctors.

Ruth Challis said gently: 'Is it true that you're going to marry Clive Mortimer? The juniors have been buzzing with the news of your engagement all the morning.'

Jessica smiled wryly. 'Yes, it's true.' She pinned on the clean white apron, adjusted her cap in the mirror and checked that she had notebook and pen in her pocket in readiness for report.

Ruth had not believed the circulating rumour for it had seemed to her that Jessica was more attracted to Lester Thorn than to Sir Lionel's exuberant and rather superficial Registrar. She did not like Clive Mortimer but she understood his appeal for the junior nurses. Most girls of Jessica Brook's age and experience had outgrown the youthful adulation, however.

'You've known each other for some time, of course,' she said.

Jessica nodded. 'Ever since my days with Sister Tutor on P.T.S.' Again that wry little smile. 'I fell in love with him then along with half a dozen other juniors. I seem to have stayed the course. All the others fell at various fences.'

Ruth laughed. 'You're obviously the faithful kind.'

'Or just bloody stubborn,' she murmured to herself as the other nurses on the afternoon shift came crowding into the room to don caps and aprons and to bombard her with eager questions and congratulations.

Later, as Ruth finished the report and gathered up her papers and the other girls rose from their chairs and drifted away to begin the various tasks allotted to them, she leaned forward to touch Jessica's arm. She smiled at her and said quietly: 'You do know that you have my very best wishes for your happiness, Jessica.'

She was touched, surprised by the warmth of the words. She had not felt that Ruth liked her very much. But perhaps she was relieved by the news that she was going to marry Clive and so would have no more to do with Lester Thorn. They were friends and she was obviously fond of him and his recent interest in another woman must have caused Ruth a good deal of heartache, Jessica thought with regret.

'Thank you. That's very nice of you,' she said in some embarrassment and moved away to begin her quota of work on the ward.

'What's all this, then?' demanded Mrs Ully in mock indignation from the chair beside her bed, the skimpy dressing-gown scarcely covering her ample charms. 'Thought you was off men!'

Jessica paused, smiled. 'Oh, you've heard.'

'That DJ fella announced it this morning. We all 'eard it.'

She stared in surprise. 'Which DJ?'

'The one what does the requests for us in the 'ospital. He said you was getting married to one of the doctors. Is it that dark chap you was talking to the other day? Ever so good-looking. No wonder you wouldn't 'ave my old man!' She screamed with laughter.

'I'm marrying Mr Mortimer. He's one of the doctors on Sir Lionel's team,' Jessica told her absently. She picked up the chart from the bottom of the bed. 'But why are you still here, Mrs Ully? I thought you were going home this morning.'

'Got a germ in me water, love. I was ever so bad in the night. Sister had to get doctor to give me an injection,' she declared proudly. 'Mortimer, eh? That's a bit of a mouthful, gel!' She patted Jessica's hand, beamed at her. 'Good luck to yer, anyway. I 'ope you'll be very 'appy.'

'Thank you, Mrs Ully.' Jessica returned the chart to its hook and walked on down the ward, thinking of the old adage that everyone loves a lover. Everyone was so pleased for her ... even a cynical old bird like Mrs Ully who never had a good word to say for her husband and constantly warned the nurses against marriage.

She wondered why she could not be more pleased for herself. She loved Clive. From her earliest days at Hartlake, she had only wanted two things ... to be a good nurse and to marry Clive. Well, she knew she was the first—and soon she would walk down the aisle to become Clive's wife. What more could she want?

She knew an odd little pang for the might-have-been when she came out of a side-ward and saw that the Professor's round was in progress and Lester was one of the group about the patient's bed. She hurried along to the sluice to lose herself while he was on the ward. Like everyone else, he must have heard that she was engaged to Clive. She was reluctant to face him for she had been wrong to encourage him even if it was not her fault that he cared so much.

The sound of running water drowned his steps on the tiles of the sluice and she was unaware of his presence until he spoke. She spun round, startled—and just a little annoyed that he was unchivalrous enough to force a confrontation in the circumstances.

'You shouldn't be in here—and you'll be missed,' she warned, wondering that he risked the wrath of the Professor by slipping away from the ward round.

'The old boy is well under way and won't notice my absence for at least ten minutes,' he said firmly.

She would not meet his very blue eyes. 'Well, I haven't ten minutes to spare even if you have,' she told him briskly.

Lester stooped slightly to look into her averted face. 'When's the happy day, sweetheart?'

The colour flooded into her oval face. That slightly mocking drawl seemed to imply that he knew as well as she did that it would be a far from happy day if she was fool enough to go through with the decision to marry Clive.

'I'm not sure ... June or July,' she mumbled, almost knocking over a specimen tube with hands that were unusually clumsy.

'A summer bride,' he commented without approval.
'Yes.'

He studied her thoughtfully. 'Sure it's what you want?' The words were low, very gentle. 'It isn't too late, love.'

'Of course I'm sure!' She wasn't—but she was not going to admit it. It was bad enough to be so stupidly unsure of what she wanted. Having made her choice she was determined to stick to it despite the odd little failing of her heart at the loving tenderness in his voice.

He was truly concerned, she thought, touched. It was not just the selfishness of the lover, wanting her for himself, refusing to accept that she could be happy with anyone else. He really did care that she should not be making a mistake. He was not asking her to reject Clive for him. He was just asking her to be really sure. He was a kind and sensitive man and he cared about people in a way that Clive never could, she knew.

'You really think you will be happy?'

'I know I will!' Her tone was emphatic. It *was* too late despite his claim. She was committed to marrying Clive—and she had every intention of being happy with him. All she had to do was forget that she had ever known Lester Thorn and that brief and exciting glimpse of a kind of loving she might never know again.

He smiled into her grey eyes but his heart was wrenched by the obstinacy and the pride which would not admit to a vanished dream and make way for a new one.

'That's all I wish for you, Jessica,' he said quietly. 'Happiness . . .' He carried her hand to his lips and pressed a kiss into the palm for keepsake. 'You'll be a beautiful bride, I know. Don't ask me to the wedding.' He turned away.

Her heart contracted. 'Lester . . .'

He paused, looked back, hope leaping.

'You'll forget me,' Jessica said, almost desperately. 'You'll find someone else.'

A crooked little smile tugged at his mouth. ' "Tomorrow's love is sweeter than today's for 'tis all promise without the heartache",' he said, quoting.

When he had gone, Jessica remained in the sluice, busily doing nothing for as long as possible . . . and trying to ignore the tears that welled in her eyes and trickled slowly down her cheeks. She did not know what she had to cry about, after all. She ought to be the happiest girl in the world!

Through the ever-efficient grapevine, she learned that Lester Thorn had taken a few days leave that was owing to him and was not expected to be seen again at Hartlake. He had resigned from his post on Professor Wilmot's team and asked for instant release so that he might take up a job in research at the Central.

It was not news to Jessica. But she had not expected him to go out of her life so swiftly. She did not know whether to be glad or sorry. In some ways, it was a relief to go about her work without the expectation of seeing him on the ward or about the hospital. At the same time, she had liked him very much and it seemed a pity that they could not have continued as friends. But they had rapidly progressed beyond the point of ordinary friendship and she doubted if they could have returned to a platonic relationship. The chemistry between them had been much too potent and no doubt it was just as well that she would never see him again.

Clive was thankful to lose a rival and sorry to lose a friend. He looked and listened carefully for any indication that Jessica was regretting the man's sudden departure. But she seemed to have settled down after that brief rebellion and she readily entered into all the plans for the wedding that they had definitely fixed for the end of June. She wore his ring on a fine gold chain about her neck when she was on duty and it gleamed on her finger at other times. They combed the local estate agents in search of a suitable property in the near neighbourhood of the hospital. She took him to Berkshire to meet her aunt and they spent a long weekend with his family in Surrey. She began to acquire a trousseau and Clive made arrangements for a honeymoon in Italy. She wrote long letters to Suzy who was to be her matron of honour and received comforting replies about the wisdom of marrying someone she had known so long and always loved. The first excitement of their engagement died down and only close friends continued to take an interest in the wedding plans.

The weeks slipped by.

Jessica told herself that she was happy and soon to be happier ... but there was a strange numbness about her heart. She seemed to have lost interest in her work and in the patients and carried out her duties almost automatically. She was not sleeping very well and she had little appetite. Rather than hurt Clive, she forced herself to respond to him while her lips and arms and body seemed to belong to someone else. If he realised her coldness, he said nothing. No doubt he put it down to reaction, pre-wedding nerves, she thought thankfully, and decided that it must be the only logical explanation for her absence of all feeling.

She entered into wedding arrangements with an indifference that she struggled to conceal. She felt as though it was another girl's wedding under discussion and it seemed completely unreal that it would be herself who walked down the aisle in bridal white on that day in June.

It was a relief when she was transferred to Keith, Male Orthopaedic. Paterson had not been a particularly happy experience for her ... and during the last few weeks she had been continually tempted to ask Ruth Challis for news of Lester Thorn. There was no harm in a friendly interest, of course—but it might be wise not to revive too many memories by talking about him. Ruth did not mention him at all and Jessica did not know if she lacked information or was merely being tactful. It was possible that Lester had severed all his connections with Hartlake. But she would have liked to know how he was getting on at the Central, she thought, a little wistfully.

She found herself working with Amanda Flynn on Keith. Their paths had not crossed for some time and she immediately noticed the change in the Irish girl. All her former exuberance had fled. She looked wan and sulky and she went about her work with a very poor grace.

She had gained a very bad report on her last ward. Sister Tutor was deploring her failure to pay attention to lectures or to work for her first-year exams. Matron had warned her sharply to remember the standards that were expected of Hartlake nurses.

For all the pert liveliness and easy-going attitude to rules and regulations, Amanda had promised to be a good nurse and Jessica wondered if heartache was to blame for the sudden decline in her work. If she had set her heart on Clive, like others before her, then she had been bitterly disappointed and when one was only eighteen that kind of thing could cast a shadow over one's entire life. Probably she felt that nothing mattered any more ... even nursing. Later, she would find that her heart was not really broken but if she was not careful it would be too late to salvage her nursing career.

She realised that Amanda regarded her with a great deal of resentment. She could not be held responsible for Clive's thoughtless behaviour but she understood the girl's feelings. She felt sorry for her. Amanda was pale and listless and much thinner than she had been. Even the riotous auburn curls seemed subdued and without lustre beneath the tiny white cap.

Orthopaedic patients required a great deal of care and attention but very little real nursing. They suffered from the pain of broken bones and the boredom and frustration of inactivity but they were not really ill for the most part. It was a busy ward and Jessica found it frustrating that Amanda went about her work with such lack of interest and irritating slowness. She was careless and slipshod and clumsy, and she appeared stupid when in fact she was a bright and capable girl when she was not indulging in self-pity.

Jessica tried to be patient, to make allowances. But she was very proud of the hospital's reputation and nurses who behaved like Amanda threatened to ruin it, she thought in exasperation when the third patient with a complaint about her called her to his bedside. Both legs were in traction and apparently Nurse Flynn had dislodged one of the weights so that he was in severe discomfort. She had also managed to spill the contents of a washing bowl over his bed while she was giving him a blanket bath. She had gone for a change of bed-linen twenty minutes ago and not come back.

Jessica went in search of the girl and found her in the deep linen cupboard, sitting on the floor with her head buried in her hands, crying like a child. She was surrounded by plastic packs of clean linen that had tumbled down on her while she was reaching for a new supply for Mr King's bed.

Despite her irritation, Jessica's heart went out to such misery. She picked up a linen pack and thrust it into the arms of a passing junior and told her to get someone to help her change Mr King's bed, taking care not to disturb the newly-set weights now that he was comfortable again.

Then she quietly closed the door and looked down at Amanda who was beginning to gulp back her sobs. 'Get up, nurse,' she said gently but firmly.

Amanda scrambled to her feet, face flaming with embarrassment, eyes bright with angry dislike for the staff nurse who had found her in tears.

Expecting a scold, she was astonished when Jessica said in friendly fashion: 'I'm sorry you're so unhappy, Amanda. Is there anything I can do?'

'Don't you think you've done enough?' The retort was savage, bitter. 'Leave me alone, can't you? I don't want to talk about it.'

Jessica regarded her thoughtfully. 'It's Clive, isn't it? I expect he made some promises that he had no intention of keeping,' she said wryly. 'I know you like him and I'm sorry that he's hurt you.'

'I don't want you to be sorry for me!' The round little chin tilted despite its trembling. 'Keep your pity!'

'I do know how you feel, you know,' Jessica said kindly. 'And of course you don't want to talk to me. I expect you hate me just now. But I do think you should talk to someone. You don't look at all well, Amanda.' The girl was emotionally disturbed and obviously her health was suffering. So was her work. She would advise her to consult Home Sister who was responsible for the well-being of the student nurses and perhaps she ought to apply for leave. It might be good for her to get away from Hartlake and all the reminders of her youthful infatuation for Clive for a little while . . .

'No, I'm not well. I'm sick to the stomach every morning,' she returned defiantly, brushing the dust from her skirts with shaking hands. 'And I can't sleep at night for worrying what will become of me, thanks to your precious Clive! I'm going to have a baby—so you can think about that when you're walking down

159

the aisle on his arm!'

The blood drained from Jessica's face and she suddenly felt very cold. 'A baby?' she echoed, dismayed. 'Clive's baby?' It was an unnecessary question. She said slowly: 'Does he know? Have you told him?'

'Of course I haven't! I haven't told anyone! I'm still trying to tell myself that it isn't going to happen!' Her pretty face crumpled suddenly and she began to cry again, despairingly.

Jessica put her arms about the anxious girl and soothed her, patting her shoulder, murmuring kindly reassurances while she wondered wryly what would become of them all. For it was impossible to abandon poor Amanda to her fate. And she could not now marry Clive, knowing that he was the father of someone else's child.

She should have been in tears herself for the selfish irresponsibility that had destroyed all their plans for the future. But, deep down, she was conscious of relief at a totally unexpected escape . . .

Clive was on twenty-four hour call that night. But he arranged for a colleague to cover for him while he met Jessica in the Kingfisher for a quiet drink when she said that she had something important to discuss with him.

He kissed her before he sat down. 'Did you like the house, darling?' he asked eagerly.

Jessica had forgotten that she had arranged to view a possible house that evening. She shook her head. 'I never went to see it.'

He took a long and grateful draught of the ice-cold lager. It was a warm evening. 'Changed your mind? Well, it wasn't a particularly pleasant area . . . and we can afford to be selective, thank goodness.' He smiled at her. 'Something will turn up soon . . . and if it doesn't, I can always move into the flat with you, Jess. There's just about enough room for us both if we take it in turns to breathe!'

She did not smile. 'When did you last see Amanda Flynn?' she asked, coming directly to the point.

Clive raised an eyebrow. 'Amanda? Lord, I don't know . . . a few days ago, I think.'

'Did you think she looked well?'

'I didn't take much notice. We didn't speak.' He grinned, wryly. 'She hasn't forgiven me for getting engaged to you, actually. There wasn't much going on between us but she made a lot of it, I'm afraid.' He looked at Jessica over the rim of his glass. 'Why? Isn't she well?'

'She's pregnant,' she said bluntly.

His eyes narrowed. 'Bloody little fool,' he said without much warmth or interest.

Jessica caught her breath at his callousness. 'Is that all you have to say?' she demanded, shocked.

'What do you expect me to say? I can't help her. She must go to her G.P. if she wants to get rid of it.'

She said coldly: 'She says that would be a mortal sin.'

'A good Catholic girl shouldn't get herself into such a mess,' he said dryly.

She was suddenly furious. 'She trusted you, Clive— and I think you're despicable to let her down so badly!'

The lager slopped over as he slammed his glass down on the table. 'Hey, hold on! What's all this?'

'She says that you're the father.'

'Well, I'm not!' he declared angrily.

She looked at him steadily. 'Can you be sure?'

A dull red darkened his cheeks. He was silent, remembering. Then he said heavily: 'No, I can't be sure.'

'I believe her, Clive.'

'What do you expect me to do . . . marry the girl?' he demanded.

Her eyes held contempt. 'I expect you to show some concern,' she said tautly. 'She's eighteen years old and she's frightened. She has to face her family—and her parish priest. Worst of all, she loves you, Clive.'

He traced a pattern on the table-top with his finger in the wet beer. 'She'll get over it,' he said, not meeting the grey eyes that looked at him with an expression in their depths that he had never seen before and did not like very much.

'Just as I did,' Jessica said quietly.

She drew the ring from her finger and laid it on the table between them. She had never liked his choice . . . the setting was too traditional, the stone too large for her simple taste. More than anything, she had felt trapped ever since he had pushed it over her knuckle with the air of royalty bestowing the accolade, she realised ruefully.

Clive looked at the gleaming diamond and then at her resolute expression. His heart sank. But he knew that nothing he could say or do would put that ring back on her finger. She had long ceased to love him, he suspected. Only habit had kept her loyal and feminine pride had pushed her into wedding plans.

He picked up the ring and slipped it into his pocket. He emptied the lager in his glass and smiled at her with an almost defiant cheerfulness. 'Wise girl,' he said lightly. 'You'd have been very miserable, Jess. I'm not really cut out for marriage.'

Jessica watched him walk from the bar and knew that he was dismayed and upset for all his bravado. He had learned to love her when she had ceased to love him. It was his turn to suffer the kind of heartache that he had inflicted on others. Because she had once loved him, she could feel a certain sympathy. But he would recover much sooner than most of those who had loved Clive Mortimer during his years at Hart-lake.

She had always known that her beloved idol had feet of clay but she had refused to admit it until it was almost too late. The boy she had known and loved, so charming and likeable for all his weakness of character, had never really grown up. He did not care for anyone or anything but himself and his ambition—and he would not allow anything to stand in the way of the latter. Certainly not a first-year nurse who had loved him too much to deny him what he wanted . . . just like herself for far too long.

She was parting with him without heartache, after all. But poor Amanda Flynn had not escaped so lightly . . .

CHAPTER TWELVE

JESSICA sat in a comfortable corner seat and watched the acres of countryside roll by . . . green and gold and brown, bathed in bright sunlight, punctuated by narrow strips of waterway and broad bands of motor-way, interspersed by isolated village and sprawling town and bleak miles of industrial city. The fast Inter-

City train was carrying her towards the Yorkshire Dales and the long-awaited reunion with Suzy.

She had missed her during the last few months. Letters and the occasional telephone call were a poor substitute for the warm affection, sympathetic understanding and lively company of her friend.

Jessica was very fond of the girl who had shared her training days. There were so many memories of the P.T.S., of silly mistakes on the wards when they were very green juniors, of fits of giggles in sluice or kitchen or linen cupboard, of loyal covering-up for each other when challenged by an irate Sister or Staff Nurse, of bemoaning the approach of dreaded exams and celebrating when they passed them, of spending most of their off duty hours in each other's company.

Suzy had been an excellent nurse, carrying off all the prizes for their year and reaching the dizzy heights of Sister at a very early age—only to give it all up for the sake of a pleasant young farmer she had nursed through a kidney transplant.

Jessica did not dislike Ian McLean. But she had yet to forgive him for marrying Suzy and whisking her off to the wilds of Yorkshire. However, they seemed to be very happy and she was glad for them.

She was looking forward to spending a week at the farm. She had hung her uniform dresses in the wardrobe and pushed her sensible black brogues out of sight and she hoped to forget all about Hartlake for a few days. She would not, of course. For Suzy would want to know all the news of the place and the people she probably missed for all her contentment with married life.

Jessica had kept to her holiday dates. She did not feel sensitive because this was the week when she should have married Clive. She only hoped that Suzy did not imagine her to be nursing a broken heart. It must be difficult for her friend to accept that she really did not wish to marry Clive when Suzy, more than anyone, had been confidante and sympathiser during years of loving. Like so many others, she probably assumed that the engagement had been broken as a direct result of Amanda Flynn's pregnancy and Clive's reluctant admission of paternity. It had been a happy release for Jessica, in truth. But to say so would have seemed like whistling in the dark and so she had followed her usual habit of saying nothing and allowing people to think what they would.

Amanda had returned to her family in Ireland and would presumably have her baby in due course. Clive had made financial arrangements for mother and child that he could easily afford and no doubt he hoped never to set eyes on Amanda again. He was still Sir Lionel's right-hand man and it did not seem that his hopes of a consultancy had been affected by the affair. Sir Lionel valued his work too highly and once Amanda had left Hartlake the whole business had been quickly forgotten, except by her particular set.

It was impossible to avoid Clive. Their work inevitably brought them together. The encounters gave Jessica neither pain nor pleasure. Some affection for him inevitably lingered but she no longer felt at all sentimental about him. Her love for him had been real enough but it had been a youthful and immature kind of loving.

All the same, it had taken a little time to settle down after so much emotional disturbance. But she was a strong-minded young woman with a sincere love of nursing and she found it possible to forget her problems while caring for those of the patients.

Gradually, the odd malaise of mind and heart and spirits ceased to trouble her and she could really look back at the events of those few weeks without regret. Perhaps she sometimes sighed for the might-have-been . . . but she would not admit it even to herself.

The bright sunshine was thrown back by golden fields, glinting steel and sparkling water as the train hummed along the miles of track. Jessica found that her eyes were a little dazzled. She turned from the window and opened her book and settled down to while away a few more miles . . .

Lester made his way towards the buffet car, thoughts of coffee and sandwiches very much to the fore as he walked through the swaying carriages. It was a popular train and most of the seats were taken. He glanced with casual interest at the occasional passenger.

The train was gathering speed after slowing for a signal and he found it none too easy to keep his balance. Lurching against one of the seats as the train rounded a bend, he put out a hand swiftly to steady himself, smiling ruefully, and looked into the grey eyes of the young woman who glanced up from her book.

He stopped in his tracks, heart turning over. For he had not expected to see her so soon. She looked very lovely in the flowered silk suit, her bright curls loosely knotted on the nape of her neck, dawning delight in the candid eyes.

'Jessica . . .' he said, pleased.

She stared at him in astonishment. One does not expect someone who is wisely kept to the back of one's mind to pop up in the flesh quite suddenly and in the most unlikely of places, after all.

166

She found that she was pleased, however. She had liked him and sometimes allowed herself to wonder how he was getting on at the Central. It had been out of the question that she should take steps to find out, of course. Having slammed the door shut with such finality it was simply not possible to hope to prise it open again. She had too much pride to run after any man!

'Hallo!' Jessica exclaimed, smiling, unable to keep the pleasure from breaking through. 'What on earth are you doing here?'

He smiled back, a little cautiously, and hoped he had not betrayed the emotion which surged through him at sight of her. He had worn his heart too openly on his sleeve in the past, he thought ruefully.

'I'm on my way to spend a few days with an old school-friend,' he said lightly. 'He has a farm in the Dales.'

'Really!' She was amused by the coincidence. 'My friends have a farm, too! I'm going to stay with them for a week. Can you imagine me—feeding the pigs and milking the cows, up to my neck in mud?' She laughed at him gaily.

'I think you'll enjoy it,' he said. The train rumbled across points, swaying. Losing his balance, he sat down suddenly in the empty seat facing her. 'May I join you?' he asked wryly, eyes crinkling with laughter.

Jessica laughed, too. She leaned forward eagerly. 'It's nice to see you,' she said warmly. 'How are you these days, Lester?'

'Very well. Very busy.' He smiled into the grey eyes that were bright with a seemingly genuine interest. He was glad that she had not forgotten him entirely. Firmly he checked the leaping hope in his heart. But he felt rather more optimistic about the outcome of this impulsive trip into Yorkshire. 'We have an intensive research programme at the Central and I'm occupied with a theory of my own, too.'

'And you prefer research to the work you were doing at Hartlake?' She was curious for she had thought him so good with the patients, so genuinely caring, that it was surprising that he should choose to work behind the scenes instead of on the wards and in theatres.

He shrugged. 'The Professor wasn't the easiest of men to work with and I've always had an inclination towards research. The Central offered an opportunity at a time when I had good reason for wishing to leave Hartlake.'

A little colour stole into her face although there had been no hint of reproach in his tone. 'So you really like the new job?'

'Oh, yes. How about you? Still happy at Hartlake?'

'Still there, anyway,' she returned lightly. She closed her book and set it to one side with seeming casualness, wondering if he would notice the ringless left hand, wondering if it would interest him at this late date. He smiled at her with warm friendliness, sounded and seemed pleased to see her again. But there was nothing of the lover in his manner.

Well, it would have been foolish to expect him to go on caring all these months. There had probably been a dozen women in his life since he left Hartlake. Didn't he have a reputation for being a Don Juan, a Casanova? It was a stupid conceit to suppose that he had ever really loved her at all, she told herself firmly, stifling an odd little pang. He had walked out of her life with too light a heart. A man who really loved would have put up a fight for his happiness, would certainly have maintained an interest in her through mutual friends at the hospital and, learning of her broken engagement, would surely have been in touch if only to offer sympathy and a shoulder if needed. His failure to do any of those things proved that he had decided to forget all about her . . . and she was thankful that she had been able to put him out of her mind so easily!

'I was just going through to get some coffee,' Lester said lightly, well aware of the gesture and its significance. The absence of rings was no surprise to him. He had been kept well informed. Stifling all his natural longing, he had taken the advice of friends and given her plenty of time to straighten out her muddled emotions. Perhaps it was still too soon to re-enter her life. But he took heart from her obvious pleasure in their encounter. 'Care for a cup?'

'Yes, I would . . . thank you.' She was pleased that he apparently meant to travel for part of the way in her company. There was little point in travelling separately, after all. They had not parted on bad terms and there was no reason why they should not meet as friends.

'Something to eat? A sandwich, some cake, a packet of biscuits?'

As always, he was thoughtful. She smiled at him, shook her head. 'Just coffee, I think. Suzy is sure to have an enormous meal planned for this evening. Do you remember Suzy Preston? We did our training together and she was ward sister on Pemberton until she married earlier this year. I think you must have known her?'

'Yes, I did.' Lester rose. 'Coffee for two, then. Don't go away . . .' He made his way towards the buffet car, wondering if he ought to confess that he knew Suzy much better than she obviously knew. He would have attended her wedding to Ian if he had not been on duty that particular day.

Jessica sat back in her seat, smiling. She had almost forgotten how attractive and personable he was, she told herself, refusing to remember how many times she had conjured a vision of his handsome face and dark, curling hair and very blue eyes and that smile with all its dangerous enchantment . . .

Over the coffee, they talked easily, touching lightly on a variety of impersonal subjects. Jessica felt at ease with him, grateful that he did not once refer to their brief passion for each other by word or glance, just a little surprised that he made no mention of Clive, either. He asked her nothing about her personal affairs. She could not speak of them for fear she might seem to be hinting at regret that she had turned him down.

It was very possible that he knew what had happened and was tactfully avoiding the subject. He had been friendly with Ruth Challis and they might have been in touch after he left Hartlake. If so, then it seemed all the more likely that he had never meant any of the tender things he had said to her, Jessica decided sensibly. He had got over a temporary attraction and found someone else and felt no inclination to see her again.

This chance encounter was not likely to lead to further meetings. It was all for the best, of course. They were merely ships that, having once briefly shared the same harbour, were now destined to pass each other in the night . . .

Inevitably, they talked a great deal of 'shop' as the

miles flew by outside the train windows. She wanted to know all about his work at the Central and she was loyally pleased to hear that the recently-built and extremely modern phoenix that had arisen from the ashes of a much older training hospital could not compare with Hartlake, in his opinion. For one thing, the nurses were not as pretty, he said, smiling . . . but then they did not have the old-fashioned charm of the Hartlake uniform to enhance their attractions. He agreed with Jessica that the national uniform, adopted by so many hospitals in recent years, was probably very practical and much easier to launder but it took away the distinction and the dignity.

'Don't you have a car these days?' he asked lightly. He had not been prepared to see her on the same train that took him into Yorkshire although she had been very much on his mind that day. 'Or is it out of action?'

'I don't know this part of the world and I thought I might lose the way,' she admitted. 'It seemed more sensible to take the train . . . quicker and more relaxing, certainly.'

'"Let the train take the strain . . ."' he quoted, smiling. 'Exactly what I thought.' He glanced at his watch. 'We're due to arrive in ten minutes. I ought to rescue my luggage from the other end of the train, I guess.'

Jessica felt a pang now that the moment of parting had come. He was so nice and she had always liked him. It seemed a pity that they might never meet again. It was the strangest of coincidences that they had both travelled into Yorkshire on this particular day and on this particular train and she could not help feeling that they ought not to ignore the helpful hand

171

of Fate. But she could not bring herself to say something of the kind to him. She could not throw herself at him!

'It was nice to see you,' she said brightly, a little cool because she was afraid of sounding too warm. 'Enjoy your weekend, won't you . . .'

'Thank you. I'm sure that I will,' he returned, a little amusement glinting in the blue eyes. He held out his hand. 'Perhaps we shall see each other again. Life is full of surprises.'

She smiled but said nothing, suddenly finding that her heart was too full for words. He was so casual, so indifferent. If he really wanted to see her again he had the opportunity to arrange a meeting for the near future when they were both back in London. He made no effort to do so.

She did not allow her hand to linger in that warm but merely friendly clasp. He left her, swinging down the narrow aisle towards the communicating doors between the carriages . . . and Jessica turned her head to stare blindly at the urban sprawl that announced the approach of the town, fighting back foolish tears.

There was an emptiness in her life for all the satisfaction of her work as a staff nurse in a busy hospital. She did not miss Clive, exactly. She did miss the purpose that loving had brought to her life, the hope of a greater fulfilment than even nursing could offer. Without him, there was a void—and sometimes she wondered if any man would ever fill it . . .

Suzy had promised to meet her with the car as the farm was some miles away from the market town . . . and she looked eagerly for her friend as she went through the barrier, case in hand, resolutely not trying for a last glimpse of Lester who had probably alighted before her and was no doubt already swallowed up in the crowded streets beyond the station.

Suzy gave her a warm welcome. She hugged her affectionately. 'How are you? It's lovely to see you! You're looking pale, though, Jess. I guess you were due for a holiday.'

'I'm fine,' Jessica demurred swiftly. 'I'm just flagging after that journey. If you had to marry a farmer couldn't you have found one from the Home Counties?'

Suzy laughed. 'They don't make them like Ian outside Yorkshire!'

'How are *you*? As if I need to ask . . . you're positively blooming!' Her friend was excited, too, she thought . . . colour in her cheeks, eyes sparkling, words tumbling a little too quickly. It could not be all in honour of her visit, Jessica thought dryly. She wondered if Suzy was pregnant and bursting with the news.

'Oh, Jess, I'm so happy! How can I help but bloom?' Suzy said warmly. 'Ian is the perfect husband and sometimes I just can't believe my luck. Oh, there *is* Ian . . . by the car!'

And there too, talking to Ian with all the ease of long association while his case was stowed in the boot, was Lester Thorn . . . and Jessica stared in astonishment and a little anger that swamped the instant relief and delight. She suddenly realised the reason for that glinting amusement in his eyes when he had parted with her on the train. He had known, while she did not, that they were to meet again in the very near future! How could he tease her so! Had he realised her reluctance to part with him so finally? That was the worst of all!

173

She stopped short. '*Suzy!*' she exclaimed in reproachful accusation, suddenly realising the reason for that heightened colour, that slightly conscious flow of talk. Having known her friend for so long, she ought to have recognised the familiar signs of guilt!

'What is it . . . oh! *Lester!*' The long lashes hastily veiled the guilty look in her eyes. 'Yes . . . er, he and Ian are old friends. They were at school together, you know.'

'I didn't know.' Jessica's tone was ominous.

Suzy looked up quickly. 'I'm sure I must have told you! When you wrote to say that he'd taken you to Founder's Ball! I'm sure I did!'

Jessica couldn't recall but she felt equally sure that such a snippet of news would have stuck in her memory!

'Did you invite him for the weekend—*this* weekend, knowing that I'd be with you? Oh, Suzy, I'll never forgive you!' She was ready to turn about and take the first train back to London.

'He's been promising to spend a few days with us for ages and when he rang and said he'd come this weekend if it was okay, Ian said sure, why not, he'd be very welcome. He felt a foursome would be a good idea, more fun for you,' Suzy explained, a little anxiously. 'It wasn't planned . . . honestly!'

'Why didn't you tell me!'

'I thought you might not come.'

'You were right!'

'I wanted to see you, Jess. And you did like Lester, I know. You don't really mind, do you? It's only for the weekend.'

'I mind very much!' She stifled a sigh. 'Suzy, if you're match-making I'll wring your neck!' she declared more lightly, knowing that she must accept the situation or make it worse, determined to leave Lester in no doubt that the arrangement was not to her liking!

'No such thing!' Suzy defended stoutly. 'He's quite attractive enough to find a wife for himself if he wants one! He doesn't need my services any more than you do. Don't look so cross, Jess. He'll think you don't want him around!'

'I don't!' Jessica exclaimed tartly and without truth . . . and had no time to say more as Ian came forward to take her case and welcome her to Yorkshire. Smiling, she thanked him—and wished that she had not accepted their invitation. It seemed to her that the whole thing had been planned . . . well-meant, perhaps, but doomed to certain disaster, she thought bitterly.

It seemed that her letters to Suzy had been more enthusiastic about Lester and their brief affair than she had realised and no doubt her kind-hearted and happily-married friend thought she was doing her a favour by bringing them together again.

Fortunately, they had met on the train and so she was on her guard. Or she might have betrayed an unseemly delight at the discovery that she was to spend a few days in the close company of a man she had never expected to see again . . .

She looked at Lester with reproach. 'Wretch!' she accused lightly.

His eyes twinkled. 'I'm innocent!'

She believed him. No doubt he had been lured into Yorkshire without knowing that she would be there . . . just as she had been coaxed into having a holiday on the farm in blissful ignorance of Suzy's plans for her enjoyment! But he had certainly realised while talking to her on the train that they were bound for the same destination and it had apparently amused him to keep silent.

'And I thought it was coincidence!' she declared wryly.

The two men sat in the front. Suzy sat with Jessica in the back of the car, plying her with eager questions, pointing out various places of interest, chattering away on a hundred and one things. Jessica could not make out what the men were talking about. Old school ties, no doubt, she thought dryly.

He still wore his dark hair a little long so that her fingers itched to twine themselves in the crisp curls on the nape of his neck. She had always liked the back of his neck. He had nice ears, too ... a good shape, set close to the head. His shoulders were broad and he held himself very erect. Ian tended to slump slightly over the wheel, she noticed. Idly she marvelled that Suzy had always described the man she loved as 'handsome'. He had a nice enough face ... pleasant, good-humoured, neat-featured. But he was nondescript in comparison with someone as strikingly attractive as Lester Thorn. Against her will, she suddenly recalled the ardent yet very tender warmth of his lips on her own, the urgency of the lovemaking that had given her so much delight ... and a little shudder ran down her spine while she melted inside with a renewed longing.

'Are you cold?' Suzy asked swiftly for the sun was sliding behind the hills and even summer evenings could be chilly in the Dales.

Jessica shook her head, smiled. Lester turned to look at her. She refused to meet his eyes, fancying not for the first time that he had the power to look right into her mind and heart with that intense blue gaze.

The farmhouse nestled in a small hollow, a picturesque place that had been in Ian's family for gener-

176

ations. Jessica was enchanted by her dormer bedroom with its pretty chintz curtains and bedcover, its welcoming bowls of roses from the garden, its attractive views across the meadows and down to the river.

She washed her face, applied fresh make-up and brushed her hair, unpacked her case, and then went down to join the others in a drink before they sat down to an excellent chicken casserole and rice pudding that Suzy had put in the oven before leaving for the town to meet the train. Plain fare but quite delicious, accompanied by some very nice wine, Jessica decided as they dawdled over coffee in lazy contentment.

During that short respite in her room, she had realised that she must treat Lester with casual and lighthearted friendliness, knowing that he would follow her lead. Fortunately, they were on friendly terms. If Suzy had any hope that they would ever be more than friends again then she was doomed to disappointment, Jessica felt. For Lester was courteous and very pleasant and quite charming and she enjoyed the evening more than she had expected to do. But there was not the slightest hint of the lover that he had been all those weeks before. She was almost tempted to believe that she had imagined his ardent pursuit, his eager wanting and her own willing surrender . . .

CHAPTER THIRTEEN

THE days passed too quickly.

Lester, surprisingly adept, had great fun trying to teach her to milk a cow. Quite unnecessarily, of course, as Ian's pedigree herd were milked by a very efficient machine in the scrupulously hygienic dairy.

Jessica scored when it came to riding. As a child, she had competed in gymkhanas with her own pony. She was quite fearless on the back of Ian's restive black stallion, equally at home with the heavy old Shire who was ending his days in the meadow near the river's edge and whinnied with pleasure at her approach. She fed him with apples and endearments and he ambled happily about the meadow with her on his back while Lester leaned on the gate, observing her child-like delight and her natural empathy with the horse. Wearing shirt and shabby jeans, hair flying loose and her fair skin already kissed by the sun, she looked very different to the cool and competent staff nurse of Hartlake Hospital.

He had never seen her quite so relaxed, so carefree. She was happy, enjoying the company of friends and the simple delights of country life and the superb weather. She was certainly not a broken-hearted bride mourning the might-have-been as her wedding-day dawned and passed with no wedding, he thought thankfully, looking carefully for the slightest shadow in the grey eyes, the slightest droop to that lovely mouth. His deep conviction that she had never really loved Clive Mortimer was confirmed all over again.

She and Suzy were like a couple of teenagers when they were together, talking non-stop of remembered times, giggling over the least thing, sharing secrets ... delightful and enchanting to eye and mind and heart. It was impossible not to like the warm-hearted, friendly and very hospitable Suzy. It was impossible for him not to love Jessica.

But he did not show his love and he made no

attempt to speak of it. Before, he had spoken too soon
and laid siege with such intensity that he had frightened her away. She was a woman who needed to be
coaxed and not compelled into loving. But gentle per-
suasion took time and much patience . . . and the need
of her had tormented him for weeks. However, he set a
fierce control over himself. Suzy knew her so much
better than he did. Suzy's advice must be sound.

He had expected the weekend to be something of a
strain. Instead, he found that he could relax, too. Jessica's attitude towards him was light but warm and
friendly, not exactly encouraging but far from discouraging. It conveyed liking and some pleasure in his
company but there was no hint of coquetry. Lester
suspected that she was physically stirred by him but
that could be an instinctive response to the chemistry
that had always existed between them. Without
mutual love, it was meaningless. She gave no hint of
wanting him and he had no intention of alarming her
with amorous approaches just when she was relaxing,
trusting him, offering him the warmth of an affection
that might lead to loving with time.

They swam in the river and basked in the sun and
tramped for miles across the Dales. They walked and
talked in perfect amity, almost forgetting Ian, busy on
the farm and Suzy, cleaning house and baking and
tending her garden and quite content to allow her
guests to wander off by themselves. Hartlake and the
Central were not exactly forgotten for they talked
much about the work that was so important to them
both. But it seemed very remote from that lovely part
of the world.

They were golden hours, golden days . . . and they
passed too quickly.

With only a few hours left before he must take the train to London, Lester lay on his back, dozing in the warm sun, his dark hair still wet from the swim and clinging in tight curls about his neck and ears.

Jessica lay on her stomach beside him, toying with a long blade of grass. Ian and Suzy were down by the river. The remains of their picnic tea were spread on a rug, surrounded by piles of clothes and shoes and books and the transistor radio which still played softly in the background.

She studied Lester, secure in the knowledge that he was unaware of her intent gaze. She committed every line of his handsome face to memory and to her heart as though she dreaded never to see it again. For the first time, she noticed a few silver threads against the dark of his hair. There were laughter lines about his eyes, slightly deeper lines about his mobile mouth. Jessica felt a little rush of warm tenderness for him.

All through that lovely weekend, he had kept his distance. She marvelled that so much eager passion should have died so complete a death. She was woman enough to know when a man did not want her, she thought ruefully. He had held her hand, walked with her and talked with her, lifted her over stiles and across streams and looked upon her in the briefest of summer clothing without apparently feeling a flicker of the former desire. So it could not have been a lasting love that he had felt for her, she reasoned with a little heaviness of heart. It could only have been the bright flame of passion that leaped . . . and then died.

He had made no demands on her at all during the weekend. He had not even hinted at their past intimacy. It might never have happened. It was good that they could be friends with no shadow of the past to mar the relationship, she told herself firmly. It proved the quality of this man that he could treat her with respect and warm friendliness when she had given herself to him with a haste that another man might have despised.

They had been lovers too soon, she thought, remembering that headlong response to his touch that had swept her so unaccountably into his arms when he was little more than a stranger. It had been all wrong . . . and yet it had felt so *right*!

Jessica was aware of a growing ache in her breast, the constriction of tears in her throat. She suddenly wanted to lay her head on his chest and know his arms about her once more, his lips on her hair, the soothing murmur of loving words. She longed for his kiss, his embrace. She needed him to love her!

He had loved her once . . . and she had sent him away, told him to forget her, to find someone else. He was not the kind of man to cling to an empty dream. He had been strong enough to overcome the weakness of his loving, his wanting . . . and she must not expect him to love again just because she wished it. Now, she was nothing more than a friend. They would never have met again if Suzy had not manoeuvred these few, glorious days for her sake. He had been content to make a new life without her, it seemed. She must not expect to call him back to her side just because she was lonely and a little lost.

She had been so sure that she loved Clive, that her feeling for this man could only be physical attraction. She *had* loved Clive—with the unquestioning devotion of the very young. If he had been a different kind of man, it might have matured into real and adult loving. She had needed that glimpse of the true to recognise the false, she thought sadly—and then she had been too proud, too obstinate, to admit that the new love was greater than the old . . .

Lester was awake, very much aware of her. It took all his self-control not to reach out a hand to her, draw her close. But he was determined that if she wanted him then she must make the first move. Pride had kept her from him in the past. Her love would have to be greater than her pride or it was worthless to him.

His heart beat heavily for he sensed her mood. This might be the last few moments that they would have alone before he caught the train back to London. If she let him go without giving him one small sign that she needed him as he needed her, then it was the end, he felt. Desperately he willed her to say something, do something, while there was still the time and the opportunity. One word, one touch of her hand, one small reaching-out for the happiness he knew that they could find together!

Almost of its own volition, her hand moved towards the dark head, the lean cheek. His name trembled on her lips. Her breast swelled with the ache of loving, the dread of parting with no promise for the future. About to lay her hand against his cheek in gentle caress, to say his name with longing, moved by a deep need that cancelled out everything but her love for him, she saw Suzy's shadow fall across them and knew it was too late. The moment had gone. Pride returned in force and she scrambled to her feet and went to help Suzy and Ian to pack up the picnic.

Lester did not stir for several minutes. It took that long to accept, to come to terms with defeat. She was too sensitive not to have been aware of the tension of those few moments when he had sent out all his love and longing in silent prayer. He was forced to face the truth that it was not pride but her complete failure to love that stood between them . . .

Jessica had never known such desolation of spirit as the train carried him away and out of sight, possibly out of her life. Her only keepsake was the brief, almost impersonal kiss he had bestowed on her cheek as a perfunctory courtesy. He had kissed Suzy with more warmth, she thought heavily.

Afraid to be silent, for Suzy could be too perceptive, she talked of a hundred and one things during the drive back to the farm that evening, careful to make the occasional light reference to Lester with as much naturalness as possible.

Suzy was not deceived. 'You'll miss him,' she said quietly when Jessica finally paused for breath.

'Lester? Oh, I don't think so. I'll have more time to spend with you,' she said brightly. 'He did monopolise the weekend, don't you think?'

Suzy turned to look at her with sceptical eyes. Jessica leaned forward to look more closely at a quaint old cottage at the side of the country road.

'I've never seen anyone so much in love and so determined to deny it,' Suzy said, sighing.

Jessica forced a little laugh. 'Being married has turned you into a romantic, sweetie! I like the man well enough and I admit that he's very attractive. But I'm certainly not in love with him!'

'You're certainly a liar,' Suzy retorted. She reached to pat the slim hands that were entwined so tightly in Jessica's lap that the knuckles shone white. 'That foolish pride will condemn you to a lifetime of nursing and nothing else if you don't take care, Jess,' she warned gently.

Her mouth twisted wryly. 'He said once that I was bloody stubborn.'

'So you are! Don't you want him, Jess?'

She was very pale. 'Yes.' Her voice was low as she reluctantly admitted the truth to the friend who cared and would not betray her. 'You know that I do, Suzy. But I've made a mess of things. He doesn't want *me* any more.'

Suzy stared. 'You aren't just proud and stubborn,' she declared. 'You're blind as a bat, too!'

Jessica shook her head. 'I was with him for hours, remember . . . entirely alone, sometimes. He never gave the slightest sign . . .' She broke off, her breast heaving as she battled with her emotions. 'Do you think I wasn't hoping, praying? Oh, Suzy, I just don't know what to do,' she said desperately. 'I know I won't see him again!'

Suzy did not answer immediately. Lester must have had very good reason for staying silent when so many golden opportunities had been offered to him, she thought. At the same time, Jessica could be so cool, so reserved, so reluctant to show her feelings that he might have been completely discouraged. At moments during the weekend, she had been tempted to shake her friend . . . and no doubt she had been anxiously keeping poor Lester at arms' length whenever they were alone!

At last, she said quietly, thoughtfully: 'Perhaps he was hoping and praying, too—for some sign that *you* care, Jess. You turned him down, after all. Not many men will offer their faces for slapping a second time— and you aren't known as the iceberg for nothing!' She could only plant a few seeds and hope that they would bring forth fruit, she thought wryly.

That view of the matter had not occurred to Jessica. She thought it over. Far from being cold and distant to him, she felt that she had come near to betraying an unbecoming warmth too many times!

She shook her head. 'He never hesitated to say that he loved me when we first met. I've never known a man with less pride! No, he just doesn't care these days—and why should he?' she said bravely. 'I slapped him hard and I daresay he's found plenty of girls to kiss him better in the meantime.'

Suzy brought the car to a halt outside the low farm-house and waved to Ian as he emerged from the dairy buildings. He liked to supervise the milking and so she had taken Lester to the station. Jessica left her friend to assure Ian that they had arrived in good time for the train and went up to her pretty room beneath the eaves.

She should have travelled back to London with him, of course. The farm and its surroundings held too many poignant memories of the past few days and she would miss him far more than if she had her work and the patients and the usual routine of her daily life at Hartlake to occupy her mind . . .

She arrived in London in the early evening, some days later. Resolutely she had refused to cut short her holiday. The weather had changed with Lester's de-parture, turning wet and blustery. It would have been an excellent excuse for returning earlier than she had originally planned. But what did she have to go home to but an empty and very lonely flat? Suzy and Ian were kind and companionable and very hospitable and the days were not really too long, she told herself firmly. But it had still been a relief when the train began its long journey to the metropolis and Suzy's waving figure on the platform slowly vanished from sight.

The terminus was very busy, filled with people who wanted to get out of the city after the week's work. Jessica pushed her way through the crowd beyond the barrier, convinced that her case weighed more than when she had set out for Yorkshire, not looking forward to the underground journey across London in the rush hour.

Someone caught her by the arm, swung her round— and she looked into Lester's blue eyes. Her heart leaped.

'I almost missed you,' he said. 'It took me half an hour to find a place to park.'

'But how did you . . . oh, of course! Suzy rang you!' she exclaimed, a little wary, wondering just what her friend might have said to him. Like too many newly-weds, Suzy was anxious to see all her friends happily married and determined to see romance where none existed, she thought wryly. 'You needn't have bothered to meet me, Lester!'

'It isn't a bother, love.' The endearment seemed to drop carelessly from his lips. Jessica wondered if he realised that it was the first time in months that she had heard that heart-warming word on his lips. He took her case. 'Come and have a drink until the traffic clears a bit. Then I'll take you home.'

She opened her mouth to protest, closed it again as she met that well-remembered look in his blue eyes. 'Thank you,' she said meekly.

The station bar was crowded, too. They squeezed into a corner and Lester ordered drinks. To protect her from the crush, he stood with an arm about her shoulders, inclining his head to hear as she babbled inanely about the train journey, the weather since he had left the farm, the various forms of entertainment that Suzy and Ian had devised to keep her happy.

She knew she was talking too much. She was so glad to see him that her heart was singing and she was desperately afraid that he would realise. He was such a kind man, so generous, so sensitive and good-hearted and she was terrified that he might take pity on her need of him—and the last thing in all the world that she wanted was his compassion when once he had freely offered his love!

One last gamble ... and it was paying off, he thought exultantly. She could not hide that look in her eyes when she saw him. He had not given her time, deliberately surprising her. She could not keep the warmth from her voice for all the banality of the words she uttered. She could not help the slight tremble of her body as she stood close to him no matter how hard she tried to keep that barrier of seeming indifference between them.

Suzy had not betrayed any confidences. She was not that kind of person. She had only suggested that it might be a good idea to meet Jessica's train if he could ... and he had continued to follow her advice although it had not availed him very much so far. At times, he had felt that if he obeyed his own instincts he might be spared many weeks of heartache and loneliness and near-despair. He had never lost his belief in Jessica's love for him although it had taken a devil of a time to reveal itself! Now he felt that he was nearer to happiness than he had been for too many months. But he was not going to rush things. He could play it just as cool as Jessica if that was how she liked it!

They finished their drinks and left the bar and

walked some little way to the side-street where he had left his car.

Jessica did not take much notice of the route they were taking. Her heart had quietened and she was thankful that she had kept her head. For his presence at the station and this comfortable journey to her flat was just one more example of his kindness and consideration. She must not assume anything more than that.

He stopped the car outside a cottage-style house in a narrow street that dated from the early part of the century. It was vaguely familiar. Then she remembered. 'Isn't this where you lived when you gave that party months ago?'

He nodded, leaned across to open the car door. 'I still live here.'

'I thought you must have moved to the other side of London when you went to the Central,' she said slowly.

'Were you interested enough to find out?' His tone was a trifle brusque but not accusing. He swung himself out of the car and she followed him to the front door, wondering but willing to fall in with any plans he might have.

He ushered her into the narrow hallway and she walked on to the lounge. Memories came flooding as she looked about the room that had been filled to over-flowing with people when she first saw it. Now she looked about her with interest, admiring his taste in furnishings and paintings, reading the titles of some of his books.

He called to her from the kitchen.

A very appetising smell reminded her that she was hungry. She looked at him in amused surprise. 'Do I get fed, too?' For a small table had been laid for two and he was busily taking the chill off a bottle of wine.

He smiled at her. 'I'm not much of a cook,' he warned. 'I just throw everything into a pot and call it goulash.'

Suddenly, all her defences were down. Perhaps he did not love her any more. But she loved him—far too much to go on being lonely and miserable when one small move might take her into his arms and that heaven she had found with him before. What did it matter if it did not last? At least she would have a few more memories to cherish, to take out and look at in quiet moments between attending to the many needs of her patients in the years to come . . .

She went to him and put her arms about him and pressed a kiss into the hollow of his neck. A pulse throbbed beneath her lips. She felt a wave of love, of tenderness, of engulfing need that swept away all her pride, her obstinacy, her foolish refusal to admit that her love for him was greater than anything else in her life.

He held her very close, stroking the soft blonde curls. 'It's only goulash,' he said lightly. 'You haven't tasted it yet. You might not be so grateful when you do!' he joked but his heart was very full. For she had come into his arms just as he had always hoped that she would. She was ready to give with all her heart and it had been worth the long and painful waiting.

'Idiot,' she said softly, moving away to look up at him. 'It isn't gratitude. It's love.' She said the words without embarrassment or shyness or false pride. She smiled at him with a wealth of commitment in her grey eyes.

'Of course it is,' he told her gently. 'But I thought you were never going to accept it.' He kissed her, very tenderly. 'You're so bloody stubborn, Jessica love . . .'

Doctor Nurse Romances

Don't miss
February's
other story of love and romance amid the pressure
and emotion of medical life

NURSE SMITH, COOK
by Joyce Dingwell

Nurse Fiona Smith has looked after her young
nephew ever since his mother's death — and is determined to continue doing so after his father insists he
joins him in Australia. But the boy's father stipulates
'no accompanying women' so on arrival she pretends
to be his new cook instead . . .